Auld
Acquaintance

Auld Acquaintance

SOFIA SLATER

Swift

SWIFT PRESS

First published by Swift Press 2022

1 3 5 7 9 8 6 4 2

Set in Minion by Tetragon, London
Printed in England by CPI Group (UK) Ltd, Croydon, CRO 4YY

A CIP catalogue record for this book is available from the British Library

ISBN: 9781800750470
eISBN: 9781800750487

For Theo Saplund

Should auld acquaintance be forgot
And never brought to mind?
Should auld acquaintance be forgot
And days of auld lang syne?
For auld lang syne, my dear
For auld lang syne
We'll take a cup o' kindness yet
For days of auld lang syne

30TH DECEMBER

CHAPTER 1

There was an arm hanging out of the car window. You might have thought its owner was out for a summer drive, window rolled down to catch the breeze. But the ambulance came right up behind my taxi as we were passing. I craned my neck to see. Then I wished I hadn't. There was blood all over the shattered glass, like syrup staining shaved ice.

It was a hard sight to put out of your mind, but then there wasn't much to distract me once I got on the ferry. The sky and the sea threw off dull grey light, the same shade as the boat's paintwork. The horizon was interrupted with little crenulations of coastline. Without the green of summer, or the dramatic shafts of sunlight, it looked nothing like the pictures that had so appealed to me weeks earlier, when I did an excited image search for 'the Outer Hebrides'. I watched one of the ferrymen, his high-vis jacket a shocking splash of yellow in the otherwise grey scene, running a broom up and down an exterior wall. Maybe this was a vital task in the effort to keep things shipshape. Or maybe he was as bored as I was. I was really bored.

My mind kept jumping back to the accident. That, too, had been the only thing to look at in a sparse landscape, with dawn slowly revealing the wintry hills and scattered houses on my early ride from the hotel to the ferry port. I had clung to my cup of sad machine coffee, cadged from the bleary girl on the desk as I checked out, and wondered, *How do you crash that badly into a little roadside ditch?* It was an odd place for it, and that oddness, as much as the upsetting possibilities of injury and death, gave the six-hour journey ahead an ill-starred feeling.

I had to try and shake it off. Six hours is a long time to stare at a grey horizon, feeling doomy, but more than that, I *had* to enjoy this weekend. This party was my turning point, the beginning of a better year. New Year, new me. When Nick's invitation came in November, it had been the first good thing to happen in ages. *Can I tempt you?* ran the subject line, which was intriguing enough, especially coming from someone I hadn't spoken to in months. Someone I missed.

Hey Millie!
Long time no write. I know this is out of the blue, and it might not be your kind of thing anyway, but… I'm going to this New Year's Eve bash with some friends, and one of them had to drop out. Should auld acquaintance be forgot and never brought to mind? In your case, no! There's no

one I'd rather take a cup o' kindness with than you, so please come, if you can stomach the journey.

Nick x

And then, below his name, the invitation: neon tartan and a bunch of stag silhouettes, and the words 'Party like it's 1899'.

You are cordially invited to an exclusive Hogmanay celebration on the Isle of Osay, to be held in Fairweather House. You make the journey, we'll do the rest. Whisky, bonfires, Scottish baronial vibes.

Hearing from Nick made a warm thrill travel up my spine. I looked up pictures of the island, which appeared luxuriously streaked with purple from the summer heather, and the house, a neo-Gothic Victorian pile. It was the only thing there, apparently: some old laird's retreat, just a speck among the larger Hebrides.

Getting there was a nightmare. The ferry ride was long and the boat left before dawn, only on weekdays. That was after you had trekked the length of the country to reach the port. The house looked like it would be freezing in winter, too. But I wasn't really debating whether to go – it was enough that Nick had thought of me, months after we stopped working together. Even if nothing was going to happen there, it would still be a laugh. And much better than what I had planned: binging on leftover Advent chocolates and Christmas specials until I fell asleep at ten o'clock. I replied that I'd be delighted, journey be damned.

And now here I was, on 30th December, shivering on the northern swell. I'd had a brutally early, undercaffeinated start, the weather was shit, and I'd just seen a car crash; none of this was cheering, certainly. But neither, I reminded myself, were these omens of anything. It was just bad luck. I went to the toilet to dab my face with a damp paper towel and give myself a talking-to in the mirror.

When I emerged, we were making the first of our two stops, at a bigger island on the way to Osay. A few people got off, and a small crowd of men and women in heavy jackets gathered on the quayside to pick up supplies. We'd been going for a couple of hours now. If I looked behind us, I couldn't make out the mainland any more, not so much as a charcoal smear on the horizon.

As we chugged slowly on towards the next island, I got out my binoculars and notebook. I might as well try to spot some birds on the journey, though as I focused the lenses, the sea wind bit my hands, and I wasn't sure how long they could stand the cold. But I was rewarded straight away. A barnacle goose was flying over the water towards the coast. Its elegant black-and-white face stood out glossy and fine against the grey sky. It wasn't a rarity, but unless you travelled north frequently you might not see one that often, and I still got a buzz from spotting them. I was following its movement, mesmerised by the beauty of its curling wingtips, when something yellow crossed my lens and I lost sight of the bird.

Lowering my binoculars, annoyed, I saw the cause: the long blonde mane of a woman about my age – maybe a year closer to thirty, I reckoned – contorting against the handrail to get a selfie. There was something familiar about her. She tried a few different pouts and angles, then called out:

'Ravi, babe, I need you!'

A man leaning against the wall of the passenger cabin, whose glossy black quiff was just as gallingly perfect as her beachy waves, looked up from his phone and crossed the deck.

'Can you get some of the island? The weather is giving me *nothing*.'

I turned away, rolling my eyes. Not as privately as I thought, though. A man in a red anorak was leaning on the opposite rail, and he gave me a crooked smile, jerking his head at the well-coiffed couple.

I could feel myself blushing, and I moved off down the deck, hiding my embarrassment behind the binoculars, hoping the cold wind would be an adequate excuse for red cheeks if he was still looking.

I adjusted my lenses and thought about what my dad would have said. 'Keep breathing, smoothly and quietly. If you aren't calm, the birds won't come.' He died when I was thirteen, but I still reached for the things he'd taught me when we went birdwatching. Those times were so peaceful – just him and me, walking through woods or along the seaside, binoculars bouncing against our chests, companionably silent, reaching over to tap each other on the shoulder and point to a movement on the horizon.

After he was gone, and I was living with my mother, it was just me in the woods, scoping the sky, pretending he was around the next tree. I was tired of it being just me.

I didn't spy any other birds of note – a seagull here, a tern there – and by the time we pulled away from the next stop, it was too dark to keep looking. It was intensely cold, too. I ducked into the passenger cabin and tried to rub my stiff fingers back to life.

Inside, the Well-Groomed Couple were tapping their screens, and the man who had smiled at me from the guardrail, hands tucked into his jacket, leaned his head against the wall, eyes closed. There was only Osay ahead of us now, so these people must be going to the party, too, and I felt even worse that I'd been caught out in my annoyance. It occurred to me that Nick should have been on the ferry too, but perhaps he'd gone a couple of days ahead. I didn't recognise any of them as people I'd seen him with, though I was still trying to place the blonde's features. She was *definitely* familiar. Perhaps it was only her style, though – the blonde waves, prayer beads and crystal pendants reminded me of my mother, also given to a certain Californian aesthetic that she hadn't been born into.

I felt too awkward to start a conversation, even though I knew we were headed to the same place, so I sat gingerly at the end of a bench and started blowing on my fingers. Down the length of the wall, Red Anorak's eyes flew open, and he flashed another crooked smile.

'Hey.'

'Hi.' It emerged as a hoarse whisper. I cleared my throat, embarrassed, realising that, apart from muttering, 'Checking out. Coffee?' to the girl on reception at the hotel, I hadn't spoken to anyone all day. Not that that was such a rare occurrence for me lately. I tried again. '*Ahem*. Hello.'

'Scottish baronial vibes?'

'How'd you guess?'

'Not many left on the boat. I'm James.' James was six feet or so, a bit past thirty, not particularly handsome, unlike the other two in the cabin, but with a face I wanted to keep looking at. He seemed cheerful and healthy, outdoorsy, though maybe that was just the anorak.

'Millie. Nice to meet you.' I reached out to shake his proffered hand and was embarrassed all over again when my own, reddened by the cold, refused to uncurl. But he took it anyway and started rubbing it between both of his.

'You want to be careful with those things. Frostbite can be serious. Birding?'

The touch felt like a big move. It startled me, and made me wonder when the last time I'd touched anyone was. But I didn't pull my hand back.

'Uh… yeah,' I stuttered.

'Binoculars gave you away. Figured either birdwatcher, or peeping Tom. Seeing as there's not a lot to peep at on the sea…' He smiled at me, but the crooked corner of his mouth uncurled when he saw my face. 'Only joking.'

'No, it's…' I nodded to where his hands were still enclosing mine.

'Oh! Sorry. Should have asked.' He relinquished them. 'I work at a hospital. You get sort of used to just focusing on the ailment. Not a lot of boundaries.'

'That's okay. They do feel better.' I waggled my fingers to demonstrate. 'So, you're a doctor?'

'No, nothing so impressive. Pharmacist.' He gave a good-natured laugh, but it was a little rueful, too, as if he'd had to answer the question a few too many times, and it hadn't stopped stinging. 'I've dabbled in twitching, though, like you.'

I was more of a birder than a twitcher. I'd never really gone chasing after sightings – just kept an eye on the birds around me. Though I did have a life list; and probably knowing the difference in the first place made me a twitcher by default. I let it pass without correcting him.

'Oh yeah?'

'I've never really caught the bug, but I do a lot of outdoor sports, and you can't help but start noticing the things around you.'

So, he *was* outdoorsy; I hadn't just imagined it. Now I saw he had a slightly weatherbeaten look, in a good way: hazel eyes glinting out from the kind of embedded tan that lasts through the winter. I was about to ask what his most impressive sighting was, when someone else spoke.

'So, you two are going to this party, yeah?'

It was Well-Groomed Male, calling out from across the cabin. He was leaning back on the bench, one loafered foot, bare at the ankle, crossed over the opposite knee. Well-Groomed Female was still on her phone, but she flicked her eyes up at us as James answered.

'We are. Fellow revellers?'

'Yes, mate. Should be epic. God, I wish they'd told me it'd be so fucking freezing, though.'

He pulled down the cuffs of his waxed jacket performatively. I wouldn't have thought anyone needed to be told that socks are a good idea if you're visiting Scotland in December.

'I'm Ravi, and this is Bella.'

The blonde looked up while we introduced ourselves.

'Do either of you know the owners? I'm setting up a post, but I don't know what mentions to use.'

'Sorry. I'm a plus one.' I knew I sounded a bit too pleased from the look she gave me, but I couldn't help it when I thought of Nick's message.

'Same here,' said James.

'Whatever, I can take the personal angle for now and leave partnerships out of it,' she said. Then, after thinking a moment: 'But Rav, we need to talk to someone about this when we get in.' She turned back to the phone.

Of course. Now I knew who she was: Bella B, a rising influencer whose face had drifted across my various feeds a few times. She gave off a much more focused energy in person – that's probably what had thrown me off. Her posts were all floaty hair and diaphanous garments, sage bundles and sunset beach yoga. The oversized puffer jacket she wore may have been in a tie-dye print, but she was fiddling with her phone like a harried office worker.

'Do what you got to do, babe. I'm here to party,' replied Ravi.

The tannoy crackled into life and a harsh, indistinct announcement was made.

'Looks like it's time,' said James.

The boat bumped into something and came to a halt. I cupped my hands to the glass of the cabin window and looked out into the night. A lamp cast jaundiced light over a plank jetty, stretching off into the dark. The light was swinging in what seemed like a cold wind – it made the pier look seasick, and suddenly I didn't want to get off the boat and trust myself to it, especially as I couldn't see where it led. But then I spotted it – away above a blank blackness was a single illuminated pane. Not an extravagant beacon, but still a welcome sign of the waiting house. We had arrived.

CHAPTER 2

I was expecting some sort of greeting party on the jetty, a sign for the house, at least some lights along the path up the hill. Or Nick, ideally. But there was just that one lonely lamp, making a yellow pool on the half-rotted boards. The boat pulled away, too, taking its lights with it. A ferryman called back to us,

'Next visit on the second of January. Happy New Year!' And then he turned to coil a rope as the boat disappeared into the sea mist. It was just the four of us, the wind and the pier.

'I bet you get an incredible view of the stars out here when it's clear, away from all the lights,' said Bella. 'Perfect for a moonbathing session.'

I could imagine few things less appealing in the current temperature – or indeed in any temperature – than 'a moonbathing session', but I appreciated her attempt to take a glass-half-full approach.

'Let's get going up to the house,' said Ravi. 'It's fucking Baltic.'

Unfortunately, it wasn't so simple. For one thing, there was the luggage: Bella and Ravi had arrived with two giant hardcases apiece, as though they were moving abroad. James gallantly offered to steer one up the hill, but he had a bit of a hitch in his step and wasn't the quickest on his feet. Surprising, given his athletic appearance. The wheels kept sticking on pebbles and grass, and we lost the path more than once, stumbling over tussocks and shining our phone lights at our feet to try to find the way. None of this was helped by the mist, which drifted in thin shreds along the rocks where the island met the water, constantly altering our range of vision; nor by the constant bitter wind, which made my hands stiffen up again and my ears ache. Ravi was right: it *was* fucking Baltic.

Up at the house, when we finally reached it, things were a *little* less bleak. There was a lamp over the door, and a few outbuildings lurked around the corner, their doorways topped with similar round lights. The mist hadn't risen this far, either, and I felt better for being out of its clammy reach. I looked back at the pier, thinking how dark it had seemed up here when I was down there, with just the one glowing upstairs pane. But then I realised, following the line of sight down to the swaying dock light and back up to the building, that all the windows in the house were angled away from the landing place. *That's odd,* I thought. *You'd expect whoever built this would want to enjoy the view.* I tried to shake off my unsettled feeling. I'd noticed my thoughts getting darker since work went pear-shaped, and I didn't want to get in the way of my own enjoyment this weekend.

'All right, seriously, where is everyone?'

My attention snapped back to the door, where Ravi was pressing the bell for what must have been the third time.

'Probably already partying,' said James. 'I'll check round the back.'

'Cool.' Ravi sat back on his suitcase. Bella, too, was resting on hers, tapping at a photo, trying different filters. She didn't even look up. I could feel my annoyance at them welling up. How had they managed to put themselves in the position of being waited on by strangers? I didn't fancy standing with them for ages while James hunted around for someone to open the door, so I jogged down the curving stone staircase after him, calling:

'Wait, I'll come with.'

'Oh, good.' He flashed a smile. 'I didn't want to say, but I'm afraid of the dark.'

'Don't worry. I'll protect you.'

Although we were both joking, the dark *was* a little frightening. It was pitch black apart from the lighted doorways. All of them standing around in the blank night somehow reminded me of a stage set, a series of entrances anyone might suddenly walk through. Our feet were silent as we crossed the grass, and in the distance you could hear the monotonous crash of water on the rocks. Wingbeats pulsed above our heads – an owl, roosting in one of the outbuildings? The silence seemed thick, a presence more than an absence. I started chattering over it.

'So, what brought you here for New Year's?'

'Well, it seems like a pretty legendary party, doesn't it? Not often you get a chance to go all out in style this far from civilisation.'

'True. No neighbours to call the police. Speaking of, did you see that accident on the way to the ferry this morning?'

'Oh God, yeah, the couple?'

I hadn't realised there were two people in the car, but it must have been the same one. How many accidents could there have been between the hotel and the port?

He carried on, jerking his head back towards the front door where Ravi and Bella were waiting:

'If only it had been those two, right?'

I gave a little snort of assent, though immediately felt it was harsh. Sure, they'd annoyed me before they'd even opened their mouths, and I was hardly the person to rush to their defence, but I didn't want them *dead*. Still, if they came down with food poisoning for the rest of the trip...

'You meeting someone here?' I asked.

'Uh... yeah, I was invited by – aha! Here we go.'

We had come most of the way around the main building, and there was a lit window on the ground floor in front of us. An old woman's head was framed by the bright pane. Fluffy white hair caught the warm lamplight and turned it silvery. The face was hard, pinched, the mouth a red slash, compressed as she rocked back and forth, back and forth. I couldn't tell what she was doing, but out here in the dark, with shreds of mist still laying cold fingers on my shoulders, my mind jumped to the worst. That violent red mouth, and her determined gestures – it was almost as if she were sawing at something.

We approached the window, but she didn't look up until James reached out and tapped the glass. Then she screamed.

I gasped, too, and whipped my head round, expecting something to materialise out of the night. But there was nothing looming out of the dark. Then I realised: what she was frightened of was us.

Of course, I thought. *This must be the kitchen, and she's making dinner.* I could imagine the way it looked from the other side, two faces suddenly popping up out of nowhere while you were busy soaping dishes. When I looked back, the woman was holding her hand to her chest, breathing heavily, though I couldn't hear her through the glass. In the light cast by the window I could see James's apologetic gestures, pointing towards the front door.

'Go round,' she mouthed, heading in the direction of the entrance, and we moved off too. As soon as we were out of sight, both James and I let go of our suppressed laughter.

'Poor old biddy.'

'You nearly gave her a heart attack.'

The woman was saying exactly the same thing, in a reproachful tone, to Ravi at the open front door when we rounded the corner. Her querulous, frightened manner was at odds with the knife handle poking out from her apron pocket. Or perhaps she'd brought it along for protection.

'I don't quite understand you,' Ravi was objecting.

'I'm so sorry, I didn't mean to startle you,' James called out as he started up the stairs.

'You could have rung the bell.'

'What, this bell?' said Bella, pressing a manicured finger to the button and waiting pointedly as the long chime echoed in the hall.

'Well,' sniffed the woman, 'I'm afraid I didn't hear you.' But she yielded a little, stepping to one side so that we could come through.

In the large hall, she stood looking at us, still a little hostile, and we all stared back at her. Close up, I could see her mouth wasn't as harsh a line as I had thought. It was soft, and turning slightly inward with age – she might have been around seventy. Her lipstick made it dramatic, though: bright red, crookedly applied. Vivid blue shadow was smudged over her eyelids. The same mix of sloppiness and theatre was visible in the clothes she wore under her stained apron, a fuchsia velvet dress marred by bald patches where it had rubbed, with a slip hanging too low and peeking out from the hem.

The hall, too, had seen better days. When I had imagined it – as I had many times, thinking what I would say when I at last saw Nick, picturing a dance, maybe a little more – the surroundings had been grand, glamorous, festive. Chandeliers, caterers armed with trays of champagne, women wearing sequins, music, confetti. *This…* not so much.

The scale of the place was grand, sure, but on every other count it was a mismatch with my imagination. The ceiling extended into darkness beyond the range of vision, and cold floor tiles, set in a diamond pattern and in need of a decent scrub, stretched out into equally shadowy corners. A curved staircase, a wooden twin to the stone one outside, rose to the next floor, with portraits of kilted gentlemen hung along the landing. A tiny fire wavered inadequately in a massive hearth. The convoluted design of its carved mantel was hard to make out in the low light.

There was, in fact, a chandelier, I noticed as I craned my eyes upward once more, but it wasn't the gleaming crystal confection of my daydreams. Instead, a few sluggish yellow bulbs flickered, illuminating cobwebs draped over interlocking spears of horn: it was made of antlers, cracked and stained with age.

No Nick, either. No people at all, in fact. In all that great cobwebbed, gloomy space was just an elderly woman and the four of us from the boat. But it was only the 30th, I reminded myself. I'd arrived early. Surely it would all be transformed on the day of the party.

The woman had recovered slightly and was making an introduction.

'I am Marjorie Flyte. Fairweather House is my place. I assume you're here for the festivities?'

'If that's the word,' I heard Ravi murmur into Bella's ear, while she smirked at Mrs Flyte.

'There are supposed to be more of you, were you the only ones to get off the ferry?' she asked. The slightly querulous air she'd had when she opened the door was back again. 'Well, perhaps they're hiring a boat to come over in the morning. Some do, you know.'

I was relieved to hear we weren't the only ones. It wasn't going to be much of a party with just the five of us. But I was a little disappointed, too – I'd hoped to see Nick straight away. A clifftop walk after breakfast, though, would be nice.

'I *would* show you to your rooms, but I'm afraid the ferry was a little behind, and I'm just doing dinner. Would you mind terribly waiting in the library for now? Leave your bags and we can take them up after.' She gestured at a doorway opening off the hall. 'The others are there already; I'll call you for the meal.'

The others! My stomach flipped. So Nick *was* already here. We shed bags and coats and filed through into the other room. I tried to settle my face.

But I wasn't prepared in the least. Because it wasn't Nick sitting with a magazine on the shabby tartan sofa in the next room. My heart, which had been fluttering with expectation, began pounding with dread. I took a step back, hoping to get away, though I knew I couldn't. Nestled innocently between the sofa cushions, gently illuminated by the firelight, was someone I didn't want to see at all. Someone I'd been avoiding for a year. Someone I'd hoped never to see again.

Penny Maybury.

CHAPTER 3

'Well, clearly the ferry ride hasn't agreed with *you*.'

The comment didn't come from Penny. She was silent, looking up at me from the sofa, her face locked in the same stiff, wide-eyed blandness I could feel my own assuming. I turned to look at the speaker, a black man in late middle age leaning against the mantelpiece. The warm, uneven light of the fire showed silver hair cropped short, a well-cut suit, impeccable shirtfront and pale silk tie. His eyes were sharp under the quirked brow.

'Winston. Winston Harriot,' he said, gesturing at his tailored extent, and then opening a broad fan of fingers towards me expectantly. Before I could reply, though, the eyebrow changed its angle to express surprise, as his attention turned to Ravi, who was entering behind me.

'Ravi Gopal? I didn't expect to see you here. In fact, I didn't expect to see anyone, but at least there's a familiar face among the strangers.'

It was difficult to read his expression well in the fire's uncertain light, but I thought I saw a twinge of reluctance pass over Ravi's handsome features. Still, he moved towards Winston with seeming eagerness, arms outstretched, meaning there was nothing left for me to do but acknowledge Penny.

She seemed unchanged since I had last seen her several months ago. No, not quite. She was thinner. But her blue eyes, softly curling carroty hair, moonish face and droopy garments were the same as ever.

'Hello, Millie.' She made room for me on the sofa, but pulled her long cardigan tighter around her when I sat down.

'Hi.' I looked around at the others, hoping one of them would approach for an introduction and spare me the tête-à-tête, but Ravi was introducing Winston to everyone, and they were all busy being jocular and loud, engrossed in their interaction. 'So, did Nick invite you to this, too?'

'Not Nick, but we have a mutual friend. I think they're coming in the morning.'

'Have you seen him since… um, recently?'

'No.'

'Right.' A silence fell. I hunted for something to say, but it was Penny who filled the gap.

'You look well.'

'Not according to *him*.' I nodded at Winston Harriot. 'I guess my face lost the fight with the early start and the cold. But I'm good. Well, I haven't found another job yet. But keeping busy! You?'

'Keeping busy covers it.' She gave a tight little smile. I racked my brain, but every polite question seemed laden with significance. 'What have you been up to?' Disastrous. 'How have you been?' Impossible.

If I'd known she was going to be here, I might have prepared somehow, thought of a way to smooth things over.

You wouldn't, said a voice inside my head. *You just wouldn't have come.* But here we were. I wished I knew a way to recapture the old ease. We had, after all, been friends once.

'This place is…' I gestured around the room, meaning to say something like 'nice' or 'great', but as my hand followed my gaze, I realised neither was accurate. The room, which had earned its title of 'library' with a couple of glass-fronted cases meagrely stocked, betrayed the same neglect as the hall. The furniture was old and imposing, but in a run-down way. A sofa with a missing foot rested one corner on a pile of books. It was a large room with several settees and armchairs dotting the space and portraits of long-dead lairds lining the walls. Its back reaches were invisible, but here, where the firelight lent a little help to the few weak lamps, it was bright enough to see that the flocked wallpaper was peeling where the ceiling met the walls.

The firelight picked out something else, too – the glint of an axe, large and rather sharp-looking, surprisingly so given the general state of the place, fixed at an angle above the mantelpiece. Presumably it was a ceremonial weapon, some highland accoutrement passed down with the kilted portraits. The axe was of a piece with everything else. The whole place had an ersatz feel, as if it had been decorated by a props department. Only the dirt and decay seemed wholly authentic.

A huge, resonant crash sounded outside the library, startling me, but also saving me from having to finish my sentence. I sat there, frozen by the sound, and then our hostess came into the room, moving at a pace that suggested no emergency. She was wobbling a little, and I felt another twinge of guilt; she must still be shaken by the scare we'd given her. Maybe her trembling hands had dropped a tray. Steadying herself on the doorframe, she announced, 'Dinner is served.'

We filed back through the hall – where I noticed a big brass gong – and assembled around a long table in the room opposite the library. It was too large for the number of people. The places were set several feet apart, as if we were all hostiles in an armistice negotiation. Conversation was stilted, every comment spoken a little too loudly, to make it travel across the acres of napery. Mrs Flyte, seated at the head, sent a tureen down the line.

'What's on the menu?' asked James, ladling something intensely brown into his bowl.

'Oxtail soup.' She reached for her wine glass.

'Sorry, but I'm a vegetarian?' Bella's tone tilted up in disbelief.

'Well, then, you shall have to skip the soup,' Mrs Flyte replied, pronouncing the last three words with the kind of perfect emphasis that made me think she was worried about slurring them. I saw Ravi and Bella exchange a look just as I traded one with James. 'And the main.' She drained her glass.

'Mrs Flyte,' said Winston. 'Tell us, how did you come to be mistress of this... charming establishment?'

'I always lived in London. I love the buzz of the city, the parties, the nightlife…' She trailed off, lost in memories for a moment, and then returned to herself. Clearing her throat and attempting a brisk tone that was a little too much for her level of inebriation, she continued: 'But things change, don't they, and when the chance came to take over this house cheaply, I thought, *It's such a striking location, I can make a go of it there*. I've run it as a B&B ever since.' She topped up her glass and raised it. 'Chin-chin!'

'Oh my God,' murmured James, leaning closer to me so that he could speak low. 'She's completely pissed.'

I let out a snort of laughter in spite of myself and got a quizzical look from the other end of the table.

Looking around at the others, as our hostess circled, collecting soup plates, I was struck by the ill-assortment of the group. Tottering Mrs Flyte had been charged with throwing the kind of party I couldn't imagine she'd ever attend. Winston Harriot, with his supercilious expression and good tailoring, seemed a bit old for this kind of thing, although the paunch his jacket didn't quite disguise did imply a taste for good living. Ravi and Bella made more sense. Her online profile was an enviable and exhausting mixture of muscular attitudes struck against exotic backgrounds, artfully arranged brunch tables and laughing bunches of girls out at the kind of clubs where nobody is sick in the loo. From the conversation Ravi was having with Winston, I could tell the former worked in finance, so he probably took a 'work hard, play hard' line. His job seemed a strange pairing with Bella's digital bohemian persona, but then he *was* very good-looking. Those three had obviously met before, or at least Winston and Ravi had. But the look on Ravi's face when he first saw Winston came to me again – something weird there.

Then there was James, next to me. He hadn't met any of the others, so his friends must be arriving by hired boat tomorrow, too. Were they part of Nick's group? One of them must have money, to be coming out from the mainland so expensively – even the public ferry hadn't been cheap. And it wasn't Nick. I had worked with him at Flights of Fancy at the same time as Penny, and it's not as though careers in wildlife-protection charities bring in the big bucks.

'So, who invited you, James?'

'Oh, a friend I met through work,' he replied. He gave me a short smile, but didn't elaborate, and turned his gaze down to the table, where he was twiddling his knife. Perhaps he was hungry. Evidently, he didn't want to talk.

Which left me, again, with Penny.

I looked at her, seated on my other side. She had that fixed expression I knew from long team meetings when we used to work together, her eyes round and staring, their unblinking china blue and her curly hair giving her the air of a doll. Her gaze was locked on Ravi, a little intensely. Either she was miles away in her thoughts, or those thoughts were all about how hot he was. Mrs Flyte put a plate down in front of her and she broke the stare.

'This is one of my old standbys: stuffed cabbage. I catered exclusive events for years – dinner parties, too, when they were fashionable,' she was saying, in response to a polite inquiry from James about what she had done when she lived in London.

'That explains the delicious cooking,' said Penny quietly, pulling back a fold of the cabbage leaf in front of her to reveal some kind of pink meat studded with little vegetable chunks.

I snorted, and she smiled at me, and suddenly there was a bit of the old good feeling between us, like when we had been friends. Before… But I didn't want to think about that.

'Do you know all these people? Are they friends of Nick's?'

'I came over on the ferry yesterday with Winston. He's some kind of lawyer,' replied Penny, looking thoughtfully around the table as I had done a moment ago. 'I guess he knows those two. They must have been invited together.'

'By who? The invitation didn't say who was hosting it, and it doesn't really seem like her sort of thing…' I nodded to where Mrs Flyte was gulping down the beginnings of her second bottle. Well, the second that I'd seen. The rest of us had only one bottle to share, while Mrs Flyte kept one at her elbow.

'No, the place was hired. And she said some people on the next island come over in their own boats when she has an event, so I suppose it won't just be her tomorrow.'

'Phew. It's kind of…'

'Depressing?'

'I wasn't going to be so blunt, but… I got the impression it would be more…'

'And now you're worried that Nick has played a practical joke on you?'

I hadn't been, but now that she said it, a cold lick of doubt crossed my mind.

Nick *had* always been the office clown. What if his invitation hadn't meant what I hoped, and it was just a ruse to get me here, to make me eat this awful dinner? But no, his jokes had always been more of the schoolboy variety – changing my computer desktop image to a disgusting photo or tying Penny to her chair with the end of her cardigan. He wouldn't do something on this scale – and even if he had the ambition, where was the laugh?

I shook the worry off. Mostly.

'Anyway, I'm glad you're here,' she said. 'I've had nobody to talk to except Winston, who keeps telling me how brave I am, going for that "wan, faded look".' She did a good impression of his rather plummy tones, making me laugh and hope he wasn't looking across the table. 'So difficult to pull off unless one is terribly *thin*.'

We shared a smile again, and in the warmth of the moment I was tempted to touch on the past. 'I'm sorry I haven't called since –'

'What do you mean, "no internet"?!' Bella's voice was loud with distress, and her palms were flat on the table, as though she might vault over it in attack if the response didn't give her satisfaction.

'Well, just that. No internet. I've never bothered having it put in. There's the telephone, and the ferry, and that seems enough, really.' Mrs Flyte was clearing our dinner plates, mostly untouched – Bella had resorted to peeling the cabbage leaves from their fleshy contents. Now a ribbed glass dessert dish was placed before each of us, containing something vividly crimson, like blood on snow. I took a cautious spoonful and meringue shattered sweetly between my teeth. It was Eton Mess. Good, too. I silently thanked God.

'But we need it for work.' This was Ravi, resting a restraining hand on Bella's arm, but looking just as anxious. 'There's no mobile signal. We can't be offline for three days, we just can't.'

'It's New Year's! If you must, you can use the telephone.'

'But what if we both need it?'

'Perhaps you could form a queue.'

Penny gave me a smirk, which I returned. There was something perversely satisfying in seeing Ravi and Bella cut off from their devices and utterly desperate. Deeper down, though, I felt a rumble of disquiet. The island was already so far from everywhere. To be further isolated...

But the world hadn't forgotten us entirely; at that very instant, the landline rang.

Mrs Flyte shot a meaningful look at Ravi and Bella, and rose to stumble off towards the kitchen. We were left with each other and our lurid puddings.

'Did *you* know about this?' asked Bella in an accusatory tone.

'News to me,' said James, putting his hands up in mock expiation. 'And not very good news, either.'

'I knew,' said Winston, 'but fortunately I was born into a generation that got along just fine without the internet for years. Forgetting the outside world for a while sounds quite restful to me.'

Bella's eyes flicked to Penny and then me, expectantly.

'I didn't know,' I said. 'But I was invited kind of at the last minute. I'm not even sure who the hosts are. Are you?' I turned to Penny and to Winston, who shook their heads. 'That's weird, because we all said on the boat –'

I was interrupted by the return of Mrs Flyte. She stalked into the room, quite steady on her feet now, though her hand had returned to her chest. She didn't say anything immediately, but there was something in her face that quieted the room. A last small *tink* came from someone's spoon placed down on their dish.

'Did any of you see an accident, on the way to the ferry?' she asked.

James and I looked at each other. We both slowly nodded.

'Oh, it's terrible,' she said, sinking into her chair, suddenly sober. 'The couple who were in the car were killed... The police called me because –' She broke off for a moment, shuddering against her hand, still pressed flat against her heart. 'They were meant to be coming here.'

CHAPTER 4

No one seemed sure what to say at first. It was horrible, of course, but *for who*? Until we knew who had been in the car, our exclamations of sad surprise could only be general, and the deaths were no one's specific grief. The tragedy sat in the centre of the dining table, unclaimed. In my head the words *not Nick, not Nick, not Nick* ran on a loop, and I could see by the mixture of determination and anxiety on everyone else's faces that they too were picturing friends and mentally crossing their fingers. At last Winston spoke up, addressing the one person we could be sure had experienced some kind of loss, albeit of a petty variety.

'That puts out your bookings rather sadly, Mrs Flyte.'

'Oh, no.' She waved her hand to dismiss that minor concern, but continued, contradicting the gesture, 'Though, after all, it is too bad; I put linens in the Great Room.'

No one was asking what we were all wondering. I forced myself to speak.

'Did the police tell you what happened?'

'They weren't sure. They thought perhaps the husband fell asleep at the wheel. The ferry leaves so early, you know.'

Husband. I was relieved. So, it couldn't have been Nick. Unless… But no, when I thought of his message, I couldn't believe it had come from a married man, and I'd done plenty of casual online stalking since he and I stopped working together. If he was with someone, if he had *got married*, I would have found a trace.

It was Penny who asked the question we really wanted answered.

'Who – who were they?'

'A married couple,' answered Mrs Flyte, before speaking the two names I was least expecting: 'Drew and Lorna Strang.'

Penny's hand flew to her mouth, but it couldn't strangle her cry completely.

'I'm sorry… I have to…' She stood, clutching at herself, and hurried from the room.

'Did she know them?' asked Winston, looking around the table with a raised eyebrow. Everybody else, obviously relieved that no one they knew had died, shrugged and made sympathetic grimaces. I was struggling to clear my throat; it was as though shock had put a stopper in it.

'We used to work together. I did too. But they were… close.'

'Of course,' said Mrs Flyte. 'I didn't really think, but then of course you'd all know each other, wouldn't you? Oh, this is terrible. The weekend isn't going to plan at all. First the mix-up with Mr Harriot, then my help from the big island not showing up, and now this. I don't know how the party can go ahead under the circumstances.'

'Don't say that!' exclaimed Ravi. 'This is our New Year's. We can't let an accident stop us.'

'I don't know, Rav,' said Bella. 'It's not a good look, is it? Drinking and dancing when somebody's just died.'

'I'm so sorry,' said James to me in an undertone while the others debated how soon was too soon when it came to doing shots in the aftermath of a tragedy. 'It must be terrible for you, since you knew them.'

'It's more the shock. I haven't spoken to them in a year or so.' I paused, wondering when Penny and Nick had last spoken. 'We weren't exactly friends. But it's weird when something like this touches your life, you know?'

'Trust me, I do.'

We fell silent. At the other end of the table, Ravi and Bella were still arguing. She was concerned about 'optics', and he wasn't about to let the kind of New Year's party he felt was his due slip from his grasp. All the while, Winston watched them, smiling faintly and, whenever the discussion threatened to die down, dropping a gentle pot-stirring comment to set them off again. Mrs Flyte had her hand at her heart still and was rather urgently gulping down the dregs of the wine.

'Marjorie, let me clear for you,' James called down the length of the table. 'I didn't realise you were having to do everything without help.'

'Would you?' She gave him a shaky smile as he stood and began gathering the glass dessert dishes, all streaked with red. 'I usually have a couple of girls come over from the next island. They should have arrived this afternoon. I can't think what's happened. I need their help in the kitchen just to keep everyone fed until the ferry comes back, though I'm sure we won't have the party as planned.'

'Nothing goes ahead as planned on this island, does it?' This was Winston, whose only reply from Mrs Flyte was a cowed and guilty look.

'You said something about a booking mix-up?' I asked.

'Yes, I'm afraid that Mr Harriot was expecting to have the place to himself over the New Year. But then, when the larger party was planned, it seemed to me from the exchanges… I must have got muddled somehow, but I thought that he was a part of it. It was so silly of me. I didn't confirm that he knew about the celebrations.'

'I only realised when Ms Maybury arrived on the same ferry that I wouldn't be enjoying a solitary retreat.'

'New Year's on your own? Sounds a bit depressing,' said Ravi.

'And yet,' replied Winston, 'for those of us endowed with sufficient inner resources, it's quite the opposite.' He turned to me, continuing in a less cutting tone: 'I spend most of the year having far too good a time and paying handsomely for it, as my money manager here can attest.' He clapped Ravi on the back hard enough to draw a wince. 'At the New Year, I prefer to restore myself, in a peaceful spot somewhere, away from the noisy, banal celebrations the rest of the world engages in.

I quietly consider the year to come – with no conversation, but perhaps a little music. Speaking of which, I'd be grateful if you could provide me with a whisky so that I can retire to the library to use your record player.'

At his pointed look, Mrs Flyte rose tremblingly and went to rummage in a corner cupboard, making something clink in its dark depths.

'Oh dear, I'm afraid the whisky the girls were supposed to bring hasn't arrived yet either. Cream sherry, I have. Cherry brandy? And this crème de menthe hasn't even been opened.'

Winston groaned.

'Sherry, then, if I must.'

Mrs Flyte's bustle with the drink signalled the end of dinner. Winston clearly didn't want any company in the library; Penny had withdrawn in tears; and James was being helpful in the kitchen, which I admired, but not enough to want to join him. Bed and an early night were calling to me. Unfortunately, I was made useful in spite of myself.

'Can you maybe help me here?' asked Bella, struggling up the stairs with a safari's worth of suitcases, at the same time as I was starting towards the bedrooms.

'Sure.' I heaved on a shiny white hardcase with a tan leather handle. It weighed a ton, and I could only hoist it up one step at a time. Bella was engaged in a similar struggle. I looked past the bend in the stairs, at the upsettingly long flight that brought us to a hallway. This wasn't going to be a short hike.

'So you and Ravi know Winston, huh?'

'Ravi does. I guess they work together. But I've never met him before.'

'Do you have mutual friends or something, then? I mean, Penny and I are kind of here with the same group. Do you also know Nick? Nick Dawes?'

'No,' she panted, straining at her bag. 'It's, like, an event. I'm here for my profile, it's not a social thing.'

I was as out of breath as she was, and as annoyed by having to carry her suitcase as she was by my questions. But the whole occasion seemed stranger and stranger by the hour. I was starting to feel unsettled, and I wanted to understand.

'I didn't realise it was such a high-profile occasion.'

'Well, there must be some kind of promotion thing happening. Somebody who's involved in managing the house contacted me to see if I'd be willing to come and post some content. Ravi came along because, you know, *Ravi.*' Whilst I'd never met either of them before, I felt that yes, I knew. *Ravi.*

At last we arrived at the top of the stairs. A dim hallway stretched in both directions, weak bulbs in fake-candle sconces struggling to illuminate it. Each widely spaced lamp picked out a few details: oak panelling, portraits and taxidermised game. Limp tinsel clung to the picture frames, left over from Christmas – though whether the one just past or a festive season long forgotten was anyone's guess.

Bella paused to check herself in a large mirror just opposite the stairs. It had foxed, misty glass and a massive frame, too large for the small table it was balanced on. It leaned back against the wall at an angle that made me nervous. She ran a finger around her mouth to neaten her lipstick, looking into her own eyes and speaking to me over her shoulder.

'God, if they don't seriously smarten things up tomorrow, I am not going to be telling anyone I stayed here. I think she said Rav and I were around the corner to the left,' she continued, rattling the key she had grabbed from Mrs Flyte and obviously expecting me to follow her with the white suitcase. But I had done my duty on the stairs, I thought, and I had my own key in hand.

'Goodnight, then. I'm pretty tired after today, and the whole thing with the accident was so upsetting. You know, since I knew the Strangs.'

'Oh, right. Yeah.' Recalled to some basic level of politeness, Bella gave me a sympathetic grimace. 'That sucks so bad. But just try to think of it as a natural cycle. You know, the old year shedding its energy so the new year can be born, kind of thing.'

'Sure. Energy. That's a good point. I'll certainly *try* to think of it like that. Night, night.' And I turned and walked down the opposite branch of the hall, hoping to God I wouldn't find, after all, that my room was right next to theirs, lest I be forced to pass Bella in the corridor again.

Luckily, it wasn't. The oval brass plate attached to my keyring read: 'The Peach Room', and when I opened the corresponding door I could see why. The entire room – walls, carpet, bedspread, drapes – was decorated in shades of orangey pink, ranging from apricot to salmon by way of raw clam and spray tan. It was a horror, but a funny one, and suddenly it was too much for me, coming at the end of a tense, exhausting, fatal day. I set my back against the door and slid to the coral-coloured carpet, laughing in that hysterical way that sometimes takes the place of tears.

The thing was, though, I did want to cry. Everything here was just so quietly horrible – the sad decor, the awful food, the other people. It was a million miles from the escape I had hoped for, just another shoddy chapter in the shabby little life I had been running away from all year. A bit of glamour at New Year's: that was what I'd wanted. That, and a kiss at midnight, or maybe a bit more. And not only was the whole atmosphere dingy and disappointing, but Nick wasn't even here. On top of that, now two people were dead, people I'd worked with for years, who'd poured their heart and energy into the same things I cared about.

I hadn't seen Drew and Lorna since Flights of Fancy, the charity they'd run, shut down at the beginning of the year. Who knows how they'd changed in that time, but the people I'd known then would have been exactly what was needed to lift this whole sorry occasion to a more exciting level. They really *were* glamorous, and had seemed all the more so at a charity. Full as they are of do-gooders and the achingly sincere, the offices of charitable organisations aren't always the glitziest environments. But Lorna, splendid Lorna with her glossy mane and statement jewellery, and Drew, with his sophisticated grey temples and boyish smile – they'd stood out. And not just because they were an attractive couple. Their enthusiasm for the work was special, too. They had the kind of charisma that carries a room, or that overpowers your better judgement. I guess that's how they got so many donors.

But not any more. Now they were bodies on a slab. I saw again that limp, dangling arm, and winced at the rubber-necking curiosity I'd felt as I drove past. A few hot tears slipped out of my clenched eyelids. I wasn't laughing any more. Although I'd been avoiding them as persistently as I'd avoided Penny all year, I wished in that moment that crying could undo everything that had happened. Things had got messy, but I was desperate to see them alive again, even if it meant adding yet another awkward element to this increasingly uncomfortable house party. At least they knew how to create a convivial atmosphere.

Skrat-skrat-skrat. The scuttling sound made me jump out of my skin. *Just mice in the skirting*, I told myself. But my heart was beating quickly as I wrenched my pyjamas on, made a cursory pass with the toothbrush as I stood over the little en-suite basin (a vivid shade of cantaloupe) and hurried under the slippery peach coverlet. The sounds carried on, more of them now – scuttling and creaks in the walls, and an unfriendly wind muscling its way around the eaves. I tried to breathe evenly and ignore the sounds in the dark, but it took a long time to get to sleep. *Tomorrow*, was my last thought before drifting into an uneasy slumber. *Tomorrow* has *to be a better day*. My half-conscious mind caught the sound of a slamming door somewhere down the hall.

NEW YEAR'S EVE

CHAPTER 5

I awoke to gull screeches and sunlight mellowing the fleshy horror of my room's decor. I could begin to see how, in the right conditions, this place might be attractive, in an eccentric, decaying-grandeur kind of way. Baronial vibes. My brain shrugged off yesterday's worries like a dream. It was a tragedy, of course, and I was sad for Drew and Lorna. But I decided to try at least to start the day right. Seeing Penny and hearing about the Strangs, all on the same day, felt uncomfortable and horribly coincidental. I was being drawn into a past I'd scrupulously avoided revisiting. But then again, it made sense that Nick would have invited them, and accidents do happen.

I wanted to throw the window open and fill my lungs with the fresh salt breeze, but it wouldn't budge in its frame. I could see, looking out, that it was a beautiful day. Sun sparked off the water and picked out what colour there was in the wintry landscape. I wasn't sure, though, that the fine weather would last. The tussocks of wiry grass that clung to the island's surface were trembling in the gusty air, and farther away, where the land fell in cliffs to the sea, birds were moving with short wingbursts, sticking close to the island's edges and angling themselves protectively away from the wind.

Even if the weather did turn, I decided I wouldn't let it dispel the good mood I'd woken up in. Memories of yesterday – the car crash, the awkward dinner, the awful news about the Strangs – came flooding into my mind. But I put all that to one side. I used to know the Strangs, but I didn't any more, even if I was sorry they were dead. Like Ravi, I didn't want to let the unhappy coincidence ruin the party I'd been looking forward to for weeks. More than looking forward to, holding out for. I was hoping that today could still be a turning point. The end of a particularly bad year and, hopefully, the start of a better one. A 'natural cycle', as Bella had said. Shedding energy, or whatever.

On the bright side, Nick would arrive in just a couple of hours, and though nothing was how I'd imagined, misfortune also had a way of bringing people together. A sense of shared sorrow could so easily shade into intimacy. I pictured myself crying, much more attractively than I ever had in life, with no red nose or puffy eyes. Nick looked at me gravely, admiring my tender heart, and perhaps he would slip a comforting arm around my shoulders... *Don't be so callous*, I told myself, shaking off the fantasy. *It's a tragedy.* Still, I took care in applying my make-up, and I checked the mirror a few times to be sure the appropriately Scottish chunky pullover I'd brought wasn't playing havoc with my silhouette.

I lingered in the hall, curious to see what daylight would reveal, inspecting the withered flowers as they dropped onto side tables, and the patchy fur on the animal heads. I wandered away from the stairs, down to the end where the corridor turned. It did this on the opposite side, too. The house seemed to form an uneven U-shape, as far as I could tell. The architect must have been a more than usually fanciful devotee of the Gothic revival: every window seemed to face in a different direction, and the crossing angles of view were further confused by gables and trim.

Under the corner window was a massive chair covered in worn red brocade, bespeaking royal murders of centuries past, though like so many things in the house it exaggerated its qualities until it seemed as much a joke as an object. I kneeled on the sagging seat, looking out over the tussocky surface of the island to try and see if the window faced the same direction as my room. But I couldn't make sense of the featureless curves and hummocks of the view. The clouds, wispy and sparse when I'd been getting dressed, were already thickening, bleeding the distant waves of their blue-green tints so that the choppy sea looked leaden.

Passing the brass-plaqued doors to the other rooms, I felt myself wobble again. Behind one of them was Penny, dealing with the same shock as me. It would be worse for her. She had been so close to the Strangs. I was half-tempted to knock and offer her some comfort. But, given everything that had happened between us, maybe I was the last person she wanted comfort from. I carried on towards the stairs, dodging rickety, knick-knack-covered tables and jutting animal heads as I went.

Daylight might have toned down the particular ugliness of my room, but it was doing nothing for the rest of the house. Without the softening effects of night-time and low-wattage bulbs, every peeling bit of paint, every splintered panel, cracked tile and cobweb was plainly visible. Looking through the door to the library, I saw two sticky glasses still standing on the coffee table, presumably left over from last night. *That's odd*, I thought. *I was sure Winston was drinking alone.*

'So much to do before the celebrations,' complained Mrs Flyte, making me jump out of my skin as she bustled past me with a tray to collect the glasses.

'Understatement of the century,' I said under my breath. When she looked up at me, I smiled and replied, more audibly, 'Well, the house is already so striking.'

'That kind young man is helping me with breakfast, if you'll go through to the kitchen.'

I was guessing this meant James, since Ravi had done nothing last night to endear himself to our hostess. As I rounded the corner into the kitchen – a room bright with windows and clearly the only area in the whole house that had enjoyed any modernising attention in my lifetime – I was proved right. He was standing over the range, humming indistinctly to himself and stirring a big pan of scrambled eggs, which were just beginning to solidify into fluffy yellow curds. He flashed a smile at me.

'Right on time to butter the toast.'

I smiled and headed for the toaster that he had indicated with a nod. There was already a plate waiting, and a couple of slices jumped up ready. I popped two more in and started buttering. I was glad he'd given me this task, and not some other, more complicated part of preparing breakfast. I wasn't really much of a cook. Toast, though, I could manage.

Behind me, James carried on with his tuneless humming, while the stack of toast in front of me grew. Wholesome smells began to fill the room. We were the only ones in the kitchen, and it felt easy, domestic somehow, making food together without needing to speak. Suddenly, I didn't want Nick to arrive and disrupt… whatever this was.

But that was stupid. Nick and I had worked together for years, and I'd had a crush on him for that whole time. He had more than once made me choke on my coffee with his impressions of dowdy Penny buying a new cardigan or aggressively charismatic Drew dominating a room. I'd eaten a hundred lunches with him, I knew his sister's name and his favourite band, and this party was my chance to find out at last if he felt anything similar. I wasn't going to let a stranger get in the way of that, even if he did have twinkling hazel eyes and could make what appeared to be deliciously creamy scrambled eggs.

James turned to scoop some eggs onto one of the waiting plates behind him. I was crossing the kitchen with my piled golden toast, and then suddenly there was a metallic clang and he stumbled, spilling half the eggs across the table. I rushed forward.

'What happened?'

'Ach, it's nothing. I just don't always judge space quite so well with this thing. You don't think they'll notice this has had a wee tumble, do you?' He was looking dubiously at the eggs, scraping them back into the warm pan, but I was noticing what I'd been too distracted to see yesterday, first on the windy boat and then in the dark here on the island. That 'thing', which he'd given a ringing tap against the table as he spoke, was his right calf. As I could now see from the hollow look of his trouser leg below the knee, it was a metal prosthetic.

'I hadn't noticed before,' I said as I set the toast down and began helping him to wipe up spilled egg.

'Flattery gets you everywhere,' he replied. 'Motorbike accident when I was eighteen. Doesn't really get in my way any more, but still, you don't get quite the same spatial awareness from a metal tube as from, say, a foot.'

He spoke matter-of-factly, making me up a plate, but I still felt awkward, unsure how to respond to his revelation, or whether I shouldn't have said anything at all. I opted just to move on and was commenting on the deliciousness of the eggs when Mrs Flyte bustled in, carrying a clinking tray of dirty glasses.

'It's very difficult keeping the place tidy when I'm on my own and everyone leaves their things around willy-nilly.'

I wanted to reply that, yes, you could tell just how difficult it was, but I remained silent, shovelling eggs onto my toast and thence into my mouth.

Next to arrive were Ravi and Bella, who strolled in, still wearing their pyjamas, yawning and looking glamorously tousled and disgustingly fit. No sign of Penny yet.

'Oh, great, food,' said Ravi, falling on the eggs.

'White bread?' said Bella. 'Any sourdough maybe? Something gluten free?'

Mrs Flyte sniffed and replied, 'We don't have the same choice out here on the island. Groceries come by boat once a week.'

Bella shrugged and made herself a plate with seeming resignation, but at her first bite her eyes went wide with horror. I was ready to roll my own at whatever finicky comment she came out with next, but it wasn't the food that was bothering her.

'What the hell is that? I *cannot* be in the same space as an object with that kind of energy.' I followed her pointing finger and saw that by the back door, casually standing in the jumble of walking sticks and umbrellas contained by the umbrella stand, was a shotgun.

'Well, unless you plan to swim to the closest island, for the next two days I'm afraid you'll have to,' said Mrs Flyte, huffily stacking glasses in the dishwasher. 'Besides, it's nothing to make a fuss about. I only keep it to scare away the birds.'

Now it was my turn to be horrified. If the binoculars weren't enough of a clue, let me say it plainly: I love birds. So much so that I'd devoted my professional life to protecting them – not that I'd had much of a professional life in the months since Flights of Fancy had been dissolved. The thought of this fussy old woman standing on her back doorstep and *shooting* the rare creatures who visited these islands – British natives and migratory species from the Arctic, greenshanks, whimbrels, puffins, skuas – filled me with rage. I was swallowing a mouthful of bread and egg, ready to put my scorn into words, but before I could clear my throat and find a suitably withering way to begin, she bustled out of the room.

'I've got to get on the blower to those girls. I just don't understand why they haven't arrived. And then there are the other guests. That sky doesn't bode well. If they don't get here soon, that'll be that.'

Then she was gone, and I was left with my irritation unexpressed. I vented it by stalking to the dishwasher and dropping my empty plate into the rack in a pointed fashion, but my meaning was lost on the others. They ignored me and got on with their breakfasts.

'This is weird,' said Bella. James looked at her, concerned. 'Oh, sorry. Not the food. That's great, thanks. But, like, what kind of hotel makes the guests cook their own breakfast and eat it in the kitchen? Right? And why are there so few of us? I thought this whole thing was meant to be, you know, an *event*.'

'You're just pissed off because you can't check how many likes you got on your last post.' Bella glared at Ravi. 'Go on, admit it,' he said, laughingly, giving her a little hip check where they leaned against the counter together. She softened and smiled a little ruefully.

'Okay, fine, that's a factor. But weren't you expecting something a little more…' She waved her hand around expressively, taking in the whole dingy atmosphere.

'I know what you mean,' I said. 'The invitation seemed kind of extra.'

'Maybe not,' said James. 'It said "baronial vibes". I mean, when I imagine twenty-first-century aristocrats, their lives look a bit like this.'

'What did your friends say?' I asked James. 'Do you know the organisers?'

'Well for me it's more of a... working holiday.' He winked, as if that should mean something to me. It didn't, but Ravi chuckled around his mouthful of eggs and nodded appreciatively at James.

'What does that –'

'I don't understand it at all!' Mrs Flyte hurried into the room, all aflutter. 'I've just had the girls on the telephone, and they say that I called to cancel. But I didn't! It just doesn't make any sense.'

Ravi and Bella shifted uneasily against each other, their coordinated silky pyjamas whispering softly. I looked, for some reason, to James.

'You're sure you never called?' he asked.

'Of course I didn't!' she snapped, opening a cupboard stocked with whisky bottles and pouring herself a hefty tot. *Bit early for that,* I thought to myself. *And didn't she say the whisky hadn't arrived?* But before I could consider the implications, she had gulped one down and was pouring another.

'I know you lot probably think I'm ancient, but I only take pills for my heart. Not for my memory. Why would I cancel my help when I've got a full house? Well, when I'm expecting a full house, anyway.'

There had been a moment, before everyone arrived in the kitchen, when I was calmly buttering toast in James's easy company, when I thought this weekend might turn out all right. Good, even. But Mrs Flyte's disgruntled confusion snapped everything into focus: something wasn't right here. The dingy house, the cancelled staff, the way nobody's reason for being here added up to the same thing. It was all off. All of it.

Suddenly, I felt scared again. Something had been niggling since I arrived. I hadn't said anything, but now I had to figure it out. I needed to understand what was happening before it got worse. I opened my mouth, trying to pick a starting point from among my many questions.

But I was too late, because before I said a word the kitchen door burst open, and Winston entered. He was wearing an extravagantly long raincoat, and a cream-and-black tartan scarf thrown dashingly around his neck. But it wasn't his sartorial flair that cut off the words in my throat – it was his stricken face. We all stood there, waiting, watching him steam gently in the kitchen's heat. His mouth worked, but he seemed unable to make a sound. James dragged a chair towards him, its legs screeching across the tiles. He collapsed into it and hid his face in his hands. Mrs Flyte moved across the kitchen with the whisky bottle and her little glass and nudged his shoulder with it. He looked up and took the glass; as he swallowed, a shudder passed through his body with the spirit. We all watched him, none daring to ask what had happened. The silence ticked on. Finally, he spoke.

'I was walking along the clifftops. She must have started before me. I saw her, but I – I was too far. The girl. Penny. She jumped.'

CHAPTER 6

I'll never get to tell her I'm sorry, was my first thought. Or maybe, *I'll never have to tell her I'm sorry.*

I felt sick and paralysed, cemented to my spot on the kitchen floor, while everyone else began bustling around me, moving so quickly I couldn't keep track of them, as though I was the still centre of an otherwise blurred time-lapse photograph. When I dropped back into normal time, James was guiding me into a chair and setting a whisky in front of me.

'There was no time to stop her,' Winston was saying, loosening the scarf from around his throat. He waved his empty glass in the air, and when Mrs Flyte tottered off to refill it, looking blanched and unsteady herself, he followed her with an avid gleam in his eye, indicating that the shock had passed. Mine hadn't. My heartbeat was still as loud as the others' voices in my ears.

'What did you try to do?' asked James.

'I called out to her, but… Stupid girl.' He pinched the bridge of his nose for a moment, then knocked back the refill that Mrs Flyte had provided.

'But when was this?' There was a note of exasperation in James's voice now. 'You need to show us where. There might be time to save her.'

'Oh, no,' said Mrs Flyte. 'Jumping onto those rocks? I'm sure not. It's terribly rough, the sea. That poor, poor girl. To come to this…'

'Don't you see, we have to try?' said James.

While he, Winston and Mrs Flyte argued over the futility, or not, of trying to save Penny, I noticed that, like me, Bella and Ravi had been quiet this whole time. Or rather, they'd been discreet. They were conversing in an undertone, and Bella at least looked horribly tense. She was holding herself tightly, gripping the silky dark fabric of her pyjamas into bunches around her ribs. Ravi was stroking her upper arms over and over with steady downward motions of his hands, speaking in an urgent whisper.

I cleared my throat, and the other conversations faded.

'I was Penny's friend,' I said. 'And I think we should go and look. In case. We should have already. But even if we were sure she was… Even if we were *sure*,' I continued in a stronger voice, forestalling Mrs Flyte, who had opened her mouth to reply. 'We have to go and see. We'll need to call the police, and they'll want to know exactly what's happened.'

*

Mrs Flyte stayed behind while the rest of us battled our way through the increasing wind to the cliffs. The sun still shone intermittently, but there were fewer and fewer gaps in the clouds for it to break through. The water looked choppier and the brisk, salty air was so cold in my ears that I could hardly hear anything through the pain.

Or maybe it was the shock. I trudged across the corrugated surface of the island, following Winston, but it felt as if my legs were moving without me, as if I saw without really seeing as we went along. My mind was caught entirely in a whirl of thoughts about Penny.

She was almost certainly dead. By her own hand. Could I have done anything to save her? Could any of us? If any of us, it could have been only me. Everyone had seen her distress last night when we heard about the Strangs, but only I knew why she cared so much, only I was in a position to comfort her. But I hadn't said anything. I hadn't knocked on her door, had been too worried about awkwardness just to be a human being about it. Thudding on up the path, my legs felt leaden with guilt.

Ravi and Bella were behind me, huddled together against the wind and still speaking in low tones. They didn't look happy. Though, of course, none of us did. Maybe they, too, were wondering what might have happened if they'd tried to console her last night. But if it had been anyone's responsibility, it had been mine.

James, walking next to me, had been gently saying since we set out how sorry he was, or something – I hadn't really been listening, just thinking and walking. Now, though, his speech caught my attention.

'He's a bit chirpy, don't you think?' He jutted his chin towards Winston, up ahead.

'Chirpy' seemed to go a bit far. He had a serious enough face on. But it was true that he kept turning and waving us on, calling out things like 'Come on, chaps!' as though he were guiding us on a pleasure outing to see a particularly fine view. A flicker of rage went redly through me, but it had no time to grow, because as we came to the top of the next slight rise, I saw it: her coat and boots together in a heap, tragically small. This was the place where she'd jumped.

We all slowed and came to a stop. Ravi and Bella's conversation, already quiet, dropped fully into silence. We stared at the discarded parka, the boots tilted one against the other. I wondered, numbly, why she'd taken them off – and then realised it was an act of courtesy, the last she'd ever perform. She was making it easy for us to find the place.

'I saw her there,' said Winston, pointing to where the cliff jutted out, behind the clothes. 'Outlined against the sky. And before I could call out – I was stuck trying to think of the poor girl's name – she jumped.'

I took a few steps, paused at the pile of clothes, started again and reached the far point of the cliff, the point where she had stood, briefly, before... I took another step and leaned forward.

Penny had never been a dramatic person. There wouldn't have been room, really, in our office. Drew and Lorna had laid claim to all the available drama, what with their dominating voices, their strong colouring and their confidence. Nick took care of the humour, and that left Penny and me to be the responsible, organised ones, a rather dull pair. But spend long enough with someone, and, if they don't end up driving you crazy, they'll become a friend. Eventually I appreciated the subtlety of her ironic commentary on our work life, by comparison with Drew's impassioned pronouncements, or Nick's slapstick stunts. She was mistress of the discreet and deflating eye-roll.

If I had stood out for anything at Flights, it was for my love of birds. Penny was just an admin who wanted to work in the charity sector – in fact, we had once had an unexpectedly heated argument when she revealed that her cat wore no bell, and its bird-killing habit was of no concern to her. Nick had come to the job through science, and Drew would have done anything that gave him the leading role. But birds moved me, and comforted me; they were the lone good thing salvaged from the wreck of my childhood, and meant more to me than anything else.

After we exchanged sharp remarks about the cat, I had explained, feeling contrite:

'You know I used to go birdwatching with my father?'

She tucked her chin in: the stiffest, most minimal nod.

'Well, he and I got on pretty well. My mother – she left pretty soon after I was born, and then when he died, I lived with her. She didn't have the patience for birding.'

She had softened, and we'd made it up without mentioning it again. We both studiously avoided talking about her cat from then on.

And after that we were friends. I was the audience for her small satirical glances, whenever Lorna burst into the room, jewellery clanking, to describe the boozy lunch she'd just had with a donor. I was the one she called, sobbing down the line, after her breakup. I was the one here, now, even though we hadn't spoken in a year.

I leaned out farther, trying to see. My vision filled with oily black feathers as a small flock of shags burst screaming up from the rocks below. I flung my arms up to protect my face. They circled up and away, and when, still breathing raggedly, I dropped my hands and looked, I saw why they'd flown at me. Scattered across the rocks below were a handful of scrappy nests. And, among them, horribly still except where its legs trailed in the sloshing water below, was a body. Penny's.

CHAPTER 7

'Oh my God. Ohmygod, omigod. Rav, she's dead!'

This was Bella, her voice rising in panic. The others had come up behind me, and we were all staring over the edge, down the side of the cliff where shelves and slabs of grey rock jutted out in falling angles, one below the other, to where Penny's body lay sprawled.

'I did tell you,' said Winston. He was standing back while the rest of us crowded forward to look. I met his eyes, and he held my gaze coldly. It was me who looked away.

'Can we reach her?' I asked.

James eyed the drop.

'One of us might get down, but getting back up...'

'I'm not climbing down that, man. Look at it!' Ravi's voice was calmer than Bella's, but only just. He, too, spoke in the high pitch of near panic.

'There's no point. I doubt we can get down at all, but even

if one of us were a champion free climber, the girl's obviously dead. Look how still she is. And as Christian as it would be for us to gather up her body for a decent burial, do any of you feel capable of carrying it back up the sheer cliff? She was hardly what you'd call a slip of a thing.'

As callously as Winston had put it, I found it hard to disagree. An experienced climber might have made it down the cliff, but without equipment nobody was going to be able to haul Penny's limp body back up. Still, I felt duty-bound to object.

'It seems wrong just to leave her here. What if the sea gets rougher, and her body's washed away? We won't be able to return her to…' But I didn't finish, because, as far as I knew, Penny had no family. Who was there to return her to?

'I can think of worse ends,' said Winston, his musing tone once again entirely out of keeping with the situation. 'Dispersing into her constituent elements, rocked by waves, perhaps pecked first by the birds.'

At this, Ravi blanched, heaved, clapped a hand over his mouth, then lost the battle and turned to void his scrambled eggs and coffee onto the grass, next to the sorrowful little pile of Penny's clothes.

'Don't!' I leaped up and gathered her belongings together protectively. 'Don't get sick all over her things.'

'You don't have to shout at him,' said Bella, now angry instead of panicked. 'He's sensitive. Like a *normal* person.'

'Oh, so you think we should all be spewing to show we're in touch with our emotions?'

'Well at least some of us have them.'

'You think I don't care? She was *my* friend!'

'It's not like you're the only one who knew her.'

That stopped my next shouted reply in its tracks.

'Wait, what do you mean? You acted like you'd never seen her before last night.'

Now it was Bella's turn to look confused and lose her furious momentum.

'Yeah, well… Look, I just think you don't need to act like you're the only one shaken up by this.' She turned away from me and started gently stroking Ravi's back where he was crouched, still dry-heaving over the grass.

'Much as I enjoy the sight of two gorgons with their snakes hissing at each other,' said Winston, 'perhaps we should consider returning to the house to phone the police.' He didn't seem shaken at all. I was unsettled by his ability to give flourishes to his speech even in these circumstances.

'Come on, babe,' said Bella, hauling Ravi to his feet and glaring at me the whole time. I clutched Penny's coat and boots, unsure whether I was protecting them or they were shielding me, and we all started back down the path, stumbling over tussocks as though we were shell-shocked.

'It's awful we can't take care of the body properly,' James said to me quietly. 'I think it does you credit, trying to take that care with her clothes.' I gave him a grateful grimace as we carried on our stiff-legged way down the hill.

I looked behind me as we went, trying to pick out the spot on the clifftop where she had jumped. But without the marker of her discarded things, there was no way to tell one patch of earth and wiry grass from another. It was a horrible emptiness, somehow full of what wasn't there. My neck prickled, and I turned away.

Back at the house we clustered around Mrs Flyte, awkwardly jammed into the little cubby where the phone was kept, halfway along the passage between the kitchen and the hall. It was an old phone, with a long, plastic-coated curly cord that was tangled up in itself; there was no speakerphone function, so we all held our breath, straining to hear both sides of her conversation with the police.

All of us except Ravi, that is – he was lying on a sofa in the library, still pallid and sweaty, recovering from his experience on the cliffs. Bella had plumped the cushions around him and promised to bring him a cup of tea that would 'realign his chakras', but she had been unable to resist stopping on her way to the kitchen to listen in with the rest of us. She was holding a packet of strongly-scented herbs, and, between their odour and the shallow breathing, my head was starting to spin.

'Jumped, I said. She *jumped*... Yes.' The line was weak and crackly, and Mrs Flyte kept having to raise her breathy voice to make herself heard to the police. 'No, not on the shore side. Why would I be calling if she'd jumped five feet onto a beach? On the cliff side. You've got to send someone. She's dead.'

There followed a minute or so of rather defensive crackling.

'Well, of course I know it's not a very good time for it. Do you think it's a good time for me? I'm meant to be hosting a New Year's party, and now the Campbell girls have got in a muddle and aren't coming, so it's just me cooking for –'

I cleared my throat and gave her a meaningful look, and she recalled herself. James rolled his eyes at me, a gesture difficult to keep private in the cramped space. 'But it's terrible for this poor girl, above all… Yes, Penny was the name. Penny, um…'

'Maybury,' I whispered.

'Maybury. Age? Oh, thirty, I should say, or thereab–'

'Twenty-nine. She was twenty-nine, and her next birthday was in January.'

I broke down in tears and, like Ravi, had to go and recover in another room while they finished the call.

I didn't join him in the library, though, withdrawing instead to the kitchen to lean against the counter, staring out of the window and wiping tears from my eyes. As my vision cleared, I noticed there were birds wheeling out there, but they were too far away to distinguish in detail without my field glasses. That was a point – I'd left them in my bedroom and hadn't taken them with me to the cliffs. But what would it have mattered? I'm not sure I could have borne seeing Penny's body any closer.

Bella came in and filled the kettle, making brusque, standoffish gestures. I wanted to ask about the rest of the call, but I imagined she'd want to show off being in the know sooner or later, so I kept quiet and waited. I was right.

'So they're sending a couple of people over in a boat.' She didn't look at me as she said it, just busied herself about the infusion, her expression clouded by the rising steam with its marshy smell.

'When will they get here?'

'Three or four hours, they said, but the weather's getting worse, and as it's no longer an emergency...'

'You mean they might just not come? But if they wait till the storm's passed, Penny's body will wash away!'

'Better hers than theirs, I guess,' replied Bella, shrugging and turning away to take Ravi his restorative – or was it purgative? – brew. But something had occurred to me.

'Bella, wait.' She paused and looked back, raising an eyebrow. 'If the police aren't even sure they can risk the crossing here in order to collect a dead body, then no one's going to be taking boats out for pleasure.'

'So?'

'So, no one else is going to make it here today. The rest of the party isn't coming. It's just us.'

She'd been ostentatiously bored by listening to me until now, but, as this realisation hit home, her studiously unimpressed expression fell away, and her face dropped.

'Oh my God, you're right. *This* is our New Year's.'

I should have been insulted that she looked so crestfallen, but I was feeling the same. No more boats meant no kitchen help, leaving us to the tender mercies of Mrs Flyte's outdated culinary sensibility. No cobwebs would be swept away, no decorations would be hung. Most importantly, no other guests would arrive.

Meaning: no Nick. Seeing him had been my motivation for coming here, and now he wouldn't show up. It would just be me, alone again, only worse than I had imagined before I had got his invitation. My flat was a tip, but at least it was *my* tip, and I could relax in solitude. As things were, I had travelled hundreds of miles to spend New Year's surrounded by mildly irritating strangers in a filthy, creaking Victorian building that seemed somehow to have more draughts than windows.

But maybe it wasn't too late. I looked outside again, hoping to see clear skies. A last yellow gleam was being swallowed by swelling grey clouds. It didn't look good, but I decided I should call him. It could be that they were already on their way. And, I realised, whether they were coming or not, I should tell him about Penny's death. He was the only person left alive who I knew would care.

I turned to go and lay claim to the phone and saw that Bella had begun a dejected retreat down the corridor, holding the tea carefully in front of her. I remembered I had meant to ask her about her comment on the cliff. But it would have to wait. I wanted to speak to Nick, to hear his voice, to put an end to my painful uncertainty.

In the phone cubby, Mrs Flyte was slumped against the wall, staring at the floor with a glassy, fixed gaze. She looked grey and wrung out, taking little fluttering breaths. I had been caught up with thinking how much I was suffering, having lost a friend, being stuck here with no one of my own, as it were, but I realised now that it must be awful for her too. She was visibly frail; simply keeping the house going with half a dozen people in it must be hard work, let alone ringing the police to come and collect dead bodies.

'Are you all right?' I asked. She took a moment to turn away from her thoughts and focus on me.

'It's just such a terrible thing. And somehow I don't feel quite up to it.' She gave a quavering little laugh.

'It smelled pretty foul, but Bella has some restorative herbal brew going in the library. I'm sure she and Ravi could spare you a cup. Maybe a little sit-down would help.'

'Yes… Yes, that's an idea.' She pushed herself off the wall and made her tottering way towards the hall.

I watched her go for a moment, then took the stool she'd vacated, breathing deeply and trying to settle myself. I got out my phone to look up Nick's number, cursing the lack of reception; I'd have been much more at ease calling him from the privacy of my room. I could see Winston and James from where I was sitting, leaning together on the banister at the bottom of the stairs, speaking intently. The murmur of their voices reached me, though not the words. But if I could faintly hear them, they might be able to listen in on me. Still, there was nothing for it. I unhooked the receiver and started spinning out the number on the old rotary dial before I could lose my nerve.

It rang once, twice, three times. Then –

'Yello?'

I drew my breath in sharply, but no words followed.

'Hello, is anyone there?'

'…Nick?' I finally croaked.

'The man himself. Who's this?'

'It's Millie, Millie Partridge.'

'Oh. Millie? From Flights? Wow, haven't spoken to you in forever.'

This somehow wasn't the response I'd been waiting for, and I began to get a cold feeling in my stomach.

'I'm actually calling from Osay. I'm here already, and –'

'Osay?'

'The island, you know? Where we're going to meet for the party?'

'Millie, you've lost me.'

Not just in my stomach any more. I paused, wanting to defer the moment, but knowing it was inevitable.

'You're not coming up to Scotland for New Year's?'

'Scotland? Too far for me. I'm actually hosting in my flat. But you've gone all the way north, huh? Sounds like a real adventure!'

CHAPTER 8

I let this sink in for a moment. Then another. Or maybe a few more, because Nick was asking:

'Uh, Millie? You still there?'

'Yeah, I'm here. In Scotland. The Hebrides. An island.'

'Right… Well, that's cool. I've actually got a lot of party prep to do here, so unless there was something else…'

'Just – you didn't change your plans last minute, did you?'

'My New Year's plans? No, my girlfriend and I decided to have a party back in October or something. Why?'

'No reason. I think I've just mixed up the guest list here a little.'

'Okay, well, have a nice time! Good to hear your voice, Millie. Auld lang syne and all that.' And he rang off.

I sat back in the cubby, my blood thumping in my head, feeling as grey and weak as Mrs Flyte had looked when I'd found her a few minutes earlier.

He wasn't coming. And he'd never planned to. Someone had tricked me into coming here. A thought that kept my heart beating quickly and my mind racing as I sat there, trying to collect myself after the call. It seemed unlikely that their reasons were good.

Less frightening, but intensely disappointing, was Nick's revelation of a girlfriend. I'd been living in hope since he wrote to me, and now that was gone. I'd have no kiss at New Year's, no fresh start with someone by my side, let alone a friendly face to help navigate the rest of this hellish weekend. This was it. Just me, on my own, in this mess. A mess that I didn't understand any better after that call. The rotary dial stared at me like a round, unsympathetic eye. I shut my own against its gaze and let a few tears slip out.

As the crying calmed me, I reconsidered the conversation I'd just had. There had been something off about the whole exchange. Oughtn't Nick to have shown more curiosity about why I was calling? And, not to sound like a creep, but I had stalked him online pretty frequently since the breakup of Flights and hadn't seen any sign of a girlfriend, let alone one so serious that they were planning New Year's parties together months in advance. And then there was that mention of 'Auld Lang Syne'. Hadn't he said something similar in his email?

I got out my phone again and checked. Fortunately, I had left the invitation in my inbox, so it was already downloaded to the phone, and the lack of internet wouldn't be a problem. I say fortunately, but it wasn't by chance – the only other messages I'd got since then were Christmas marketing emails and job rejections, and I'd kept it visible as a kind of touchstone, a sign that the world hadn't forgotten me.

Only now it seemed that it had; or rather, it had remembered me with malicious intent. Something was all wrong with my presence here. I couldn't rule Nick out entirely, but if he hadn't sent that message, then who had, and why? I needed to investigate further, which meant speaking to the others.

It was only as I left the little phone cubby to go and find the rest of the party that I realised I hadn't mentioned Penny's death, or the Strangs', on the phone to Nick. I paused and considered calling him back, but a combination of suspicion and embarrassment stopped me. He had so obviously forgotten all about me – or put on such a convincing show of it – that perhaps he wouldn't care to know about the others either.

At the foot of the stairs, James and Winston were still talking, though they quietened as I neared them, greeting my approach with silence. Coming after my conversation with Nick, it stung: they were discussing things they didn't want me to hear. James looked especially pained by my presence.

'I think I'll go and investigate the kitchen,' he said after a short silence. 'Mrs Flyte looked quite peaky when she came through here. Not sure the old girl's up to cooking lunch.' He gave me a grimacing sort of non-smile and then set off down the corridor in the direction I'd just come from.

Which left me with Winston. I hadn't really spoken to him on my own before, and the way he was looking at me now – leaning on the banister with an insouciantly cocked hip and a Cheshire-cat grin, both dazzling and threatening – didn't really make me want to. I got the impression that if the first thing out of my mouth wasn't wildly entertaining, he'd throw his manicured hands up in the air and walk away. I was trying to think of a suitable remark, but he showed mercy and started the conversation himself.

'Rather ill omens for the year to come, wouldn't you say?'

'Certainly, for Penny. And the Strangs.'

'Ah yes, the Strangs. I'd almost forgotten, fresh tragedies keep cropping up.'

'It's horrible.' I shuddered a little and wiped my eyes, but he didn't seem about to offer me any sympathy. So I offered him some. 'And your holiday was already ruined, even before all this happened.'

'Yes, it wasn't exactly a welcome development, and that flighty – I'm sorry, that Flyte woman hasn't ever been able to explain the misunderstanding to my satisfaction.'

I could imagine him questioning her, with a sarcastic gaze and lawyerly persistence, and Mrs Flyte dissolving into resentful vagueness.

'Still,' he continued, 'I shouldn't have minded if the Strangs had turned up. Amusing people.'

I left to one side the insulting implication that the rest of us weren't, because the other part of his revelation was much more surprising.

'Wait, you knew them?'

'Drew and Lorna? Of course. Not terribly well, but we'd crossed paths a few times over the years. He consulted me sometimes on legal matters, to do with his different businesses and charity ventures.'

'So, was it them who organised all this?'

'A good question. I'd have assumed so, as you and I haven't any other links. But then I wouldn't have expected them to know Ravi. He'd have said so to me yesterday if he'd ever met them.'

He stood there, musing, stroking his stubble with the back of his hand. *Odd*, I thought. *I'd have had him down as being quite scrupulous about shaving.* I couldn't decide whether to tell him about my mounting worries. Everything he said confirmed my sense that there was something fishy about this whole occasion, but was he really the person I wanted to confide in? That cold amusement on the cliffs… But I'd never needed to talk to someone so much. I decided to chance it.

'I've just got off the phone with the person I thought had invited me. Only, it seems he didn't.'

Winston's gaze sharpened.

'Well now, that *is* interesting. I must get some coherent answers out of our hostess.'

I was about to try to persuade him to let me, picturing Mrs Flyte rendered even vaguer by the distressing developments of the past few hours, and feeling a stab of sympathy at the thought of her being subjected to another round of his determined questioning. But an immense clattering from the kitchen saved me the trouble.

'First, though, I perhaps ought to ensure that our rather tasty pharmacist isn't ruining the lunch. I do find mysteries so difficult to solve on an empty stomach, don't you?'

He headed off down the passage, fluttering his fingers in farewell without looking at me. I turned and crossed the chilly tiled expanse of the hall to the library.

Mrs Flyte was slumped into one of the sagging tartan sofas and barely looked up as I came in. I crossed the room to her, taking note of details it had been too dark to see last night: the way the portraits' eyes followed you around the room, for instance, or the motif of highland weaponry carved around the fireplace. Last night everything had seemed broken, dingy, inhospitable. Now, the flat grey daylight and everything that had occurred had heightened those qualities to a level that seemed actively menacing. Dangling cobwebs were not just dusty but filthy; a wonky-legged chair was not just unsteady but dangerous; the room, with its shabby, too-sparse furniture and the axe over the mantel, was not just cheerless but hostile.

I sat gingerly on an armchair adjacent to Mrs Flyte, who gave me a flicker of acknowledgement. Her colour hadn't improved in the past few minutes, although I could see from a third scummy-bottomed teacup that she had tried Bella's brew. She was breathing quite shallowly and didn't seem at all well, her make-up made even more garish by the pallor of her face.

I felt bad questioning her, but we had to know what was going on. Still, I could at least *begin* gently.

'James and Winston are taking care of the lunch, so you don't have to worry about that.'

'That's kind of them. Yes, I don't feel quite the thing.'

'It must be a terrible shock for you, something like this happening. After all, this is your home as well as your business.'

'It's always been such a quiet place. Too quiet, if anything.'

'Not a lot of custom?'

'Not as much as I'd hoped when I came up from London, no. I had such dreams for the place, a kind of idyllic retirement, and then…' She waved a limp hand around her, and her eyes drifted out of the window, where slate-grey clouds roiled over pale grey ones, and birds were struggling against the wind. I remained silent, unsure what to say in the face of this naked admission of failure and misery. 'I should have known to look in the mouth of any gift horse coming from my ex-husband.'

'He gave you this place?'

'Not gave, exactly. It was the divorce settlement. He was a rich man. We met when I catered one of his parties. He employed various younger women. You can guess the rest.' Again, it was too pitiable for me to know how to respond. 'But he made it too easy for me to get this house. I thought I was scoring one off him.' A weak gust of laughter. 'I hadn't seen the bills for repairs.'

'I don't know – it's a striking building, and an amazing location.'

'An amazing location to go potty in. Eventually you start to believe the stories.'

'Stories?'

She looked at me directly for the first time since I'd entered the room, something searching in her gaze. It held me in a tense silence, broken only by the rasping of her breath, until she said:

'Eventually you start to think it shouldn't belong to you. And that – that you're not alone in thinking so.'

This was perturbing – especially given my previous thoughts on the eyes of the portraits – but beside the point. I took a breath and dived in.

'Mrs Flyte, who booked the house for this party?'

'What? Why, the company, of course.'

'But what company?'

'Don't you know? Some sort of "immersive experiences" operation. They said you were all clients.'

'Immersive experiences?'

'Yes, sort of like high-end tour guides, they said, but for occasions. For people with no holiday plans. To be honest it was a bit beyond me, a lot of marketing speak.' Her eyes darted here and there, I assumed in embarrassment.

'But I was invited by a friend, and Winston booked the place for himself, didn't he?'

'Yes, that was a muddle. I don't think he's quite forgiven me. Such a harsh man, don't you think?'

'I wouldn't have said harsh. Perhaps a little… sharp.'

'He simply would not leave me be, even though I told him my heart was playing up. Incessant questions about the bookings, the system I use, who wrote to me to begin with. I simply had to leave the room to get away from him.'

In the face of this, I felt even guiltier about asking my own questions, but I had to know.

'But who *did* do the bookings, Mrs Flyte? I've been talking to the others, and everyone was invited by someone different. It just doesn't make sense.'

She bridled, but weakly, seemingly unable to decide between an indignant reaction and an invalidish one.

'Not you, too. Honestly, I don't know why there's so much fuss. The names were all perfectly in order. Winston Harriot, Penny Maybury, Ravi Gopal, Bella – now, what actually was her surname? It started with 'B', anyway. James Drake, Millie Partridge. And, of course, that poor couple, the Strangs. You're all here, aren't you? I don't see how either the company or myself are to blame. Everything seems to have gone to plan.'

'Yes, but *whose*?'

'Enough questions!' she hissed.

It was an unexpectedly violent reaction. Her baleful gaze narrowed and then disappeared as she closed her eyes and let her head loll on the chair.

'I'm sorry, I – I'm just trying to figure out what –'

'Spare me your efforts to play detective,' she replied, voice still full of venom, not bothering to open her eyes.

I was silenced, and again the room held only the sounds of her raspy breathing, and the quick heartbeat I could hear in my own ears.

'Mrs Flyte? Are you okay?' I eventually dared.

But she didn't answer me, because just then James poked his head through the door, smiled and announced lunch.

CHAPTER 9

We gathered around the huge dining table. In its centre sat a big metal pot full of garlicky spaghetti, wafting warm smells through the cold, musty house. The smell, and the sight of it, sending up steam next to a stack of plates and a tumbled pile of cutlery, was blessedly normal. Once again, James had managed to create an atmosphere of warm, calm ordinariness in the midst of the tension and chaos of this trip. I gave him a grateful smile as he dished out the pasta, but he wouldn't meet my eye. Whatever awkwardness had arisen in the hall clearly hadn't dissipated.

'Oh, but you haven't used a trivet,' Mrs Flyte was complaining from the head of the table. 'It'll stain the wood.'

'Sorry, I should have thought. It takes up all your attention, cooking for six. I'm amazed you run this place on your own.'

'Apparently she isn't on her own.' The others looked at me

blankly, and I rippled my fingers through the air around me. 'The house is inhabited by presences.'

'What?!' Bella set down her fork firmly enough to make the china jump. 'You're telling me there are spirits here?'

'Just repeating what I heard from the owner.'

'Delightful,' said Winston. 'Perhaps your ghost stories can beguile us until the police arrive and take us away from this… from here.' I was pretty sure that whatever he'd changed his mind about saying had involved the word 'godforsaken'.

Mrs Flyte was struggling with her cutlery, weakly twirling the pasta into her spoon. That sudden spurt of nastiness in the library had vanished, and she was once more simply a plaintive and delicate old woman. But I felt some residual nervousness as I watched her, now that I knew she had another side.

'They're the original islanders, supposedly,' explained Mrs Flyte. 'Those who lived here before the island changed hands in the nineteenth century and the owner built this place.'

'You mean there used to be a village or something?' asked Bella.

'Mmm. They resent the intrusion of outsiders, it's said.' Mrs Flyte finally managed to wrestle a forkful from the plate to her mouth, and chewed it thoughtfully while the rest of us looked at each other, half sceptical, half perturbed. 'Though I've never had problems of this order, I must say.'

'My dear lady,' said Winston. 'You surely don't mean to suggest that the deaths and mishaps of the past twenty-four hours, not to mention the booking cock-ups of the weeks before that, have been caused by ghosts?'

Before she could answer, Bella turned to him.

'I've been feeling some really bad energy since we arrived. Everything's off here. Can't you sense it?'

'I can, but I had put it down to more obvious causes. Human error, incompetence. That sort of thing.'

Indignation had brought a little colour back into Mrs Flyte's cheeks.

'I don't ask anyone to believe me about the spirits, but, after all, I'm the one who's been living here for years, in this house built over the villagers' graves.'

'Oh God.' Ravi, who had been silently wolfing spaghetti, now blenched and clapped a hand over his mouth. Bella turned to him solicitously. It was sweet, really – in spite of their shallowness and arrogance, they made a little team, always looking out for each other. Sweet, and a little jealousy-inducing.

'How long have you two been together?' I asked, once Ravi's nausea appeared to have subsided.

'Forever,' replied Bella.

'Informative, thanks.'

''Strue, though.' Ravi came to her defence. 'We got together at school.'

'There's never been anyone else,' said Bella, a smug smile capping her words.

'I shouldn't broadcast my happiness, if I were you,' said Winston. 'You'll make yourselves a target for the ghosts, hungry for the warm emotions of living hearts.'

We all stopped, forks halfway to our mouths, looking at him in shock. He smiled around the table as though he'd just announced wonderful news.

'You shouldn't say things like that, man.' Ravi's voice was nervy, wavering. 'Not in a house that might be haunted.'

'Ah, so we have more than one believer in our midst. What about the chef? James? Would you ascribe the delicious savour of this plain but well-cooked meal to any but your own hands? No ghostly presence giving an extra shake of the salt cellar?'

Winston's tone, as always, was jocular, but his ghoulish persistence made it somehow unpleasant.

'Nope, all my own culinary genius,' James replied, giving me a grin. This was confusing, after his stand-offishness of a few minutes ago.

'And you, Miss Millie? Do you believe in fairies?' I imagined he was quite a success in his field: the gaze trained on me was as sharp and cold as a steel scalpel, in spite of the warm honey-brown of his eyes.

'I'm not sure. I like to keep an open mind. But whatever the reason, Bella's right.' She looked up, startled, no doubt, at this sudden concession. 'Something's off here. I've been asking all of you, and everyone was invited by someone different. Plus, Mrs Flyte says a tourism company booked the place, claiming each of us were its clients, but I certainly wasn't. Were any of you? What about you, James? You said you were here in a professional capacity. Do you work for the company?'

Ravi snorted, and James glared at him. I looked between them, confused.

'Well?' I persisted.

'I wasn't brought here by a company, no.'

'So, who brought you? Come on, you've been ducking my questions ever since we arrived.'

The whole table was silent now, waiting, looking between me and James. My hysterical tone, at least as much as his evasiveness, had stilled them. Their eyes ticked back and forth from me to him, and his mouth worked open and closed, and still no one spoke.

Thump.

The noise, heavy and definite, made Mrs Flyte jump and give a soft cry. She put her hand to its favourite place, at her heart.

'I'll go and look,' she said. 'Probably just a door caught in a draught. Old houses make a terrible amount of noise.' She rose unsteadily and tottered from the room.

'Look,' James said to me quietly, while the others commented to each other on the disquieting sound and shot me slightly embarrassed looks. 'I'm not trying to hide anything from you. I just don't want to talk about my reason for being here in front of everyone. It's… It's a bit delicate. But I'm as confused as you are by the whole situation, I swear.'

Slightly mollified by this, I carried on the conversation in the same intimate undertone.

'So what's your theory, then?'

'Besides ghosts?' His hazel eyes gleamed at me, and I couldn't hold back a smirk. Winston looked over, and I tried to wipe the laughter from my face. 'It's a mystery to me. Maybe Mrs Flyte orchestrated the whole thing, just so she'd have some company over the holiday.'

'Are you sure her organisational capabilities are up to that sort of challenge?' asked Winston.

'Fair point. But why else would anyone want to do this?' I looked around at them all, hoping that somebody would have an answer. Everyone was silent. Nobody would meet my eye. It could just be bewilderment. Or it could be a more deliberate silence.

'I know.' James clapped his hands down on the table decisively, but his next words weren't the all-encompassing explanation I'd been hoping for. 'We need coffee. That'll help us think.'

This suggestion was taken up with enthusiasm, and for a few minutes we bustled about in harmony, clearing plates and searching cupboards for coffee, saucers, cups and spoons. Once we were settled in the library, though, all staring into our dark brew, the listless, confused, slightly mistrustful atmosphere descended again. James cleared his throat and stood up.

'I'll just go and see if Mrs Flyte would care to join us. Hopefully the ghosts haven't got her yet.'

We smiled weakly and watched him leave the room. Ravi, still looking a bit sick and forlorn, said what I'd been thinking ever since I spoke to Nick – maybe even longer, on some deeper, more intuitive level.

'I really wish we hadn't come.'

'Yes, why did you?' asked Winston. 'Shouldn't you be off managing my investments?'

Ravi winced, more deeply than I thought Winston's mild dig merited.

'I'm keeping Bells company, aren't I? Her career matters too.'

'You're getting pretty big online,' I said to Bella, trying to keep the resentful note out of my voice. 'I mean, I've seen your face pop up a few times.'

She preened.

'Yeah, it's going well, thanks. I guess audiences just really connect to my voice, my vision of the world.'

'And, uh, what is that "vision"?'

'Well, that everything's connected. It's all just energy. You know, you get what you deserve, what you put out into the world comes back to you. For instance, Ravi and I put out wealthy vibes, and we're reaping the rewards of that. Energetically, I mean.'

I couldn't help myself.

'So what, energetically, would you say you've done to end up on a freezing island at New Year's with a dead body at the bottom of a cliff?'

Bella's face was a scrawl of startled hostility, a slight defensive sneer marring the lush beauty of her mouth. I could feel her sizing me up, dismissing my challenge, explaining me away as another mousey, tragically ordinary person who envied her glamorous lifestyle. And it was true that I would have given a lot to have hair as lustrous and bouncy as hers. But my resentment wasn't really about that. It had much more to do with my mother.

I never saw much of my mother until after my father was dead. She was keen on finding herself, and it never seemed to occur to her to look near us. To be fair to her, I could tell even as a small child that we weren't the kind of thing she was looking for. It was difficult to imagine how she and my father had ever come together to make me. To put it in bird terms, she was tropical, in the parrot family, brightly coloured and voluble. My father, on the other hand, was something a bit drabber and more common: a grey little dunnock, perhaps. Domestic. Reassuring.

I suppose their shared love of nature must have brought them together, however different their styles, but things had broken down pretty quickly after I was born. I received a flying visit every year or so, between her trips to retreat centres and ashrams. I'd arrive home to the scent of patchouli and ylang-ylang hanging on the air in the hall. In the sitting room, she'd be asking my father warm questions about how we both were, at such speed that he couldn't answer. I'd be folded into her crystal-studded drapery momentarily, held at arm's length, asked my own series of quick-fire questions. There'd be a gift, usually some elaborately ugly object blessed by whatever charlatan she was following at that moment. If she had time before her next spiritual journey, she might take me out with her to get in touch with nature. Getting in touch with nature, in her world, meant either listening to her dole out increasingly slurred wisdom as she drank wine next to a smoky fire in the damp woods, or shopping for shawls.

Some children might have chased after such an elusive bohemian of a mother. I just wished she'd leave us alone.

Then, when my father died, she was saddled with me

permanently, and the intermittent gush of absent-minded affection turned into something more resentful and begrudging. I saw her all the time at first, as she moved into our house, burned a lot of purifying sage bundles, and wept over me. She was full of ideas about how to help me process my grief, which usually involved primal screams or wild swimming in the nude. She was too noisy for the one thing I did want to do, which was birdwatching. Then she got bored of waiting for me to come home from school and started taking trips again. I carried on, doing my homework and birding after school, getting the shopping with the envelopes of cash she'd left. I kept silent when she came back and let me know just how inconvenient it was for someone like her to be tied to this conformist suburban existence. I took a box of my father's things with me when I left for university, knowing she'd sell the house as soon as I was gone.

She usually emailed me when she was relocating from Esalen to Ibiza, and we still saw each other occasionally – a quick drink before she met someone else, during which she'd confide in me about the incredible colour of her new lover's aura. But we hardly knew each other. The only real trace she'd left on my life was a deep scepticism of people who claimed to be spiritual. Which was why every time Bella twiddled her pendants or explained why the current alignment of the stars was contributing to the bad energy floating around the house, I liked her a little bit less.

Still, I couldn't exactly say she was wrong. There *was* bad energy around the house, and it was getting worse by the hour. You just didn't need a crystal to see it.

*

Now Bella was describing a ritual we could perform, something to try and quiet the unquiet ghosts.

'The stuff should be here. You just need rock salt. There's rock salt in the kitchen, right? And lavender. I always carry essential oils in my bag. So, you just go through the rooms and scatter the stuff in each corner and snap your fingers like this.' She raised her arms above her head and snapped, flamenco-style. I suppressed a giggle. Winston did not suppress a raised eyebrow. Ravi, who wasn't listening, looked like he was suppressing vomit. 'Then you're golden.'

'Do you really think that will work?'

'Look, Millie, you don't have to share my beliefs. But at least I'm trying to do something. Maybe if we'd all tried a little harder, Penny would still be here.'

'What do you care about Penny?'

'We were at school together, okay? You're not the only one who knew her.'

This stunned me slightly. They hadn't seemed to acknowledge each other at all when we arrived. And not just in that frosty, obvious way, as when people who don't want to know each other try to pretend they haven't noticed. They really hadn't registered in each other's gaze. I wasn't sure I believed her. But then why would she lie about that? On the other hand, if she wasn't lying, why would she have pretended so hard not to recognise Penny?

'Oh. I'm – I'm sorry. I didn't realise.'

'Yeah, well, it was a long time ago. It's not like we stayed close. She was –'

'Bells.' At first, I took Ravi's single word for an appeal and thought he must be feeling sick again. But then I looked at him and saw a focus in his eyes that hadn't been there moments ago. His nostrils were flared, and the absent, queasy suffering that had been written all over his face was gone. That single syllable – it was more like a warning.

'Did you know the young lady, too?' I had almost forgotten that Winston was still there, listening. In spite of his distinct and rather sharp presence, he could be as subtle as a cat, sitting quietly in the shadows with shrewd eyes.

'Sure, yeah, we were all at the same school. But that's ages ago, man. It's like a different life.'

'So, if you knew the girl, and she did, too,' he nodded at me, then turned back to Ravi, 'and I know you... Then who knows our culinary friend with the leg?'

'Without the leg, you mean.' Ravi brayed at his own remark until Bella cut him off with an elbow in the ribs. 'He's not here because he knows anyone. He's, you know... *working*.'

'Ah,' said Winston, with a half-smile and a nod of understanding.

'What does that mean?' I asked. '*Working*.'

'He's a pharmacist,' replied Bella. 'It's a party. Think about it.'

I thought about it. Then I began to feel incredibly stupid.

'Wait, you mean –'

But then James walked through the door.

'Would someone come with me?' His tone was tense, his pitch a little high. 'I just found Mrs Flyte in her bedroom, and I think something's wrong.'

CHAPTER 10

Something was indeed wrong. Mrs Flyte lay extended on her bed, her neck arched stiffly back, her eyes closed and her breath rattling in and – painfully – out of her. She seemed oblivious to our presence. We had all come up and were crowding the doorway, with James standing over her at the bed. Nobody was keen to enter what was now clearly a sickroom. Finally, Winston pushed forward and stood opposite James, staring down at the barely breathing body below.

'Jesus, not again. I just can't.' Ravi, pallid and trembling, turned away and ran down the stairs, and Bella followed him, calling behind her that she'd phone the police and tell them to bring a medic, if they weren't already on the boat. I stepped softly into the room.

It was the only room I'd seen in the house that seemed to have a personal stamp on it. I mean the stamp of Marjorie

Flyte, not whichever baron or businessman had built the place and filled it with Caledonian kitsch. The blind was pulled, and it wasn't easy to discern much in the half-light, with the distracting rattle of her slow breath carrying on. I could see a folding screen blocking off one corner, with various garments in the same style as her threadbare magenta velvet hanging limply over it. There were clothes on the chair back, too, and more pushing open the doors of the tall wardrobe. The whole place was a mess, but not the abandoned and soulless mess of the rest of the falling-down mansion; it was a nest, the only homelike room in the house.

I bent over a vanity table, the mirror obscured by swags of bead necklaces. Pots and brushes were scattered over the surface, between the uprights of heavy silver picture frames. I picked them up one by one: a young Mrs Flyte, pretty, her lipsticked mouth opened wide in laughter and a cocktail glass partially eclipsing her face; a line of young women in matching aprons, proudly holding up full dinner plates; Mrs Flyte again, a little older now, her smile not so wide, but still looking happy, her eyes fixed on the large man with a moustache who had his arm round her and was talking to a child, just out of shot – you could see a small hand and the edge of some fluffy curls. Was he the man who'd relinquished the island to her in their divorce? I thought of the creaky emptiness of the rest of the house. These pictures, this threadbare velvet jumble in this one dark room – this was what remained of her life. I felt a little dart of fear travel down my spine. It was too easy to imagine my own life, years from now, reduced to one messy bedroom that only I ever entered. But I wouldn't even have pictures to remind me of a once-full life.

'Is there anything to be done for her?' Winston and James were still standing over her on either side of the bed. I took up a position at the foot.

'I found her collapsed there,' said James, pointing to a spot among the general tumble of clothes, shoes, books and crockery that made up the moonscape of the floor. 'I hoped she'd be more comfortable once I laid her on the bed, but...' We looked at her, the greying skin and unseeing eyes, the limbs tensed against agony. She certainly didn't look comfortable.

'Don't you have medical training?' I asked.

'Yeah, but I'm not a doctor. And look around, there's no equipment, nothing to help her. I think she's had a heart attack. Unless we get medical attention immediately, there's probably not much hope.'

I looked around, and unexpectedly spotted something useful. Not a defibrillator, but still.

'What about this?' I crossed to the vanity again and picked up the little pill bottle I'd spied there. I shook it and the rattle cut across the sound of Mrs Flyte's stertorous breathing. James held out his hand for the pills and inspected the label.

'It's for her heart, all right, but it's medication for a chronic condition, nothing that would help with acute failure.'

'It has to be better than nothing,' said Winston, his tone a little impatient. 'The woman's lying there dying. We'd best try. Keep looking, girl; there might be something.'

'She can barely breathe,' said James, preventing me with a gesture. 'I don't think we're going to get her to swallow anything.' Still, he opened the bottle, as though hoping to tip an answer out with the pills. Then, oddly, he sniffed the palmful of tablets. And popped one in his mouth. I cried out.

'What are you doing?! She might need those. And who knows what they'll do to you.'

'The worst they can do is ease my headache.' He held them out to me, a palmful of little round pills with a pale, pinky-orange tint. 'They're baby aspirin. They look similar to the meds she's meant to take, but I see these all the time. I know the difference.' We looked at each other, bewildered, until Winston broke the silence.

'She doesn't need anything now.' He was staring down at her, solemn and with a softer face than he usually wore. My gaze followed his, but it was my ears that understood before my eyes. While we'd been faffing about with the pill bottle, her breathing had stopped. Mrs Flyte lay back, her silvery cloud of hair picking up glints of light from the shaded lamp next to the bed. Her hands, clawed against the pain a moment ago, were loose and open at her sides. As in the picture with her husband, her face was smooth and gently joyful.

She was dead.

I found myself gulping back tears. James came around the bed and embraced me.

'It's just, it's just –' I gave up trying to speak and cried against his shoulder for a moment, grateful for the simple human contact. Then Winston cleared his throat.

'Unless Mrs Flyte had an odd habit of reusing medical paraphernalia, it shouldn't have been aspirin in that bottle.'

My sobs faded slowly into nothing as the implications of his remark sank in. James withdrew his arms from around me, and the brief moment of tearful peace was gone.

'No,' said James. 'I don't think it should have been. But who could have tampered with the pills?'

My first thought was that he could have done so. After all, he was a pharmacist, more likely than any of us to have pills with him and know the effect that switching medications would have. And he'd been in the room alone before the rest of us arrived. But then, what reason would he have to harm Mrs Flyte? And why point out the switch if he had? If it hadn't been for him, I doubt Winston or I would have realised that the pills in the bottle were wrong. Even now, he could have been fooling us; I didn't know enough to tell.

Still, even if only by association of ideas, a vague anxiety lurked in me that he *had* been the one to tamper with her medication. And it was all the more insistent precisely because I had noticed that I didn't want to believe it had been him. I liked him, and surely I couldn't *like* a *murderer*?

I wasn't sure how long we stood there, in a loose circle around the body, turning over uncomfortable ideas in our minds. Each moment felt unutterably long and full. Then Bella burst through the door.

'I've called the police again, and you won't believe it – they're not going to risk sending the boat in this weather!'

'What about a helicopter?' asked Winston.

'Yes, I asked, but they said there's only one and it's already been sent to another island for – Oh my God. Is she…?'

Winston nodded.

'Fuck.'

'That's about the size of it,' I said.

'Well now we really need the police. Ugh, I can't believe they're being so slow.'

'When did they say they would be here?' asked James.

'They don't know. They'll send people as soon as the weather allows. But what are we supposed to do in the meantime?' There was a rising wail in this final question, and I suddenly became aware of how much tension was building up in the house. Everyone was on a knife-edge, and if we didn't manage to stay calm, that edge might cut.

'There's something else you should know,' said Winston. I motioned at him, I hoped subtly, to delay the disclosure about Mrs Flyte's medication. Not that I thought we should hide it forever, of course. But Bella seemed pretty tightly wound, and I worried that sharing yet another disturbing fact with her might lead to a full-on fit of hysterics.

Winston saw my staying hand, but he didn't seem to be thinking along the same lines. He met my eyes, and I thought there was an expectant glint in his. *As though he wants to see what will happen*, I had time to think, before he carried on.

'We think Mrs Flyte's heart medication has been tampered with. It's possible someone wanted her to die.'

'What?! Oh God, ohgodohgodoh–'

'Just breathe, Bella.' This was James, dropping the bottle of pills on the vanity and crossing the room towards her. He put his hands on her shoulders and I felt a little twinge of jealousy. 'You must know some breathing exercises. I know you do. You're an expert, right? Meditation, mindfulness, deep breaths. Just take them and keep counting.'

She gulped in air, uncontrolled at first and then more steadily as she went on. I looked at Winston. One corner of his mouth kept crooking into a small, private smile. It was the same one he'd worn on the cliffs, when he looked not at Penny, fallen below, but at our reactions to the fall.

'But that means…' Bella's breath had settled now, and her brain was catching up. 'That means someone here…' I saw her eyes widen again, as the implications fell into place, and tried to pre-empt the panic.

'I know what it looks like, but it might be an honest mistake! She might have got her pills in a muddle, without anyone here intending to harm her.'

'I know it's not that. I have a feeling for these things. I think those restless spirits she was telling us about are real.'

I couldn't help it: I rolled my eyes. Bella noticed, and her eyes narrowed. At least now she was annoyed rather than hysterical.

'We need to tell Ravi what's going on. And I am *not* going to be the one to call the police again.' She turned sharply, letting her golden hair whip out from her shoulders in a gesture of scorn and dismissal that reminded me of mean girls at school. The three of us filed out behind her.

I paused at the door, looking back at Mrs Flyte, stretched still and oblivious across the bed. It seemed wrong just to close the door on her, to leave her alone to begin her process of decay. But what else could we do? Practically, we were obliged to wait for officialdom to come and sort out the body and the burial. And symbolically, none of us had known her. Who could speak any meaningful words about her life? All I had gathered about her was that she was lonely, liked a drink and could turn mean if pushed too far.

I shut the door.

CHAPTER 11

'I think we should search the house.' Bella spoke very definitely. Ravi was next to her on the library sofa, holding her hand like a lost child and nodding at everything she said.

'Yes, a search.'

'And what do you expect to find?' asked Winston.

'Well…' She seemed a bit deflated at this. 'If it *is* angry spirits, there's safety in numbers.'

'Certainly, but that's true whether we march through every room of what is, if I may remind you, a rather large mansion, or remain here at our ease by the fire which our friend James has so kindly built up for us.'

I stopped listening to their back-and-forth and started thinking about what had happened to Mrs Flyte. Every so often their words caught my attention, but then the thought of her, up there in that closed room, *dead*, filled my mind again. Her up there, and Penny on the rocks, and the Strangs in their smashed car back on the mainland. It was too many deaths in a row. The more I thought about it, the more certain I was that coincidence had no part to play here. Somebody was killing people on this island. Or, in the case of the Strangs, on their way *to* the island. But who?

I doubted very much that it was ghosts. I understood why Bella was tempted to believe that it could be. After all, if it was a person picking us off, then... But I wasn't ready to finish that thought yet. Still, even leaving aside the question of whether ghosts existed at all – which most rational people wouldn't – the Strangs had died on their way here, not actually here. Vengeful island spirits would stick to the island.

Which brought me back to the uncomfortable conclusion that it might be a living, breathing person. A person in this room with me right now.

If only it *were* ghosts.

But maybe there was another way to look at it. After all, Penny had killed *herself*. I felt another stab of horror, but this was different from the creepy thought of Mrs Flyte's body beginning to decompose over our heads. This was actual pain, at the loss of a friend I should have been able to save. Or at least, whose suffering I should have noticed earlier. I winced when I thought of myself passing by her room that morning, not stopping to offer her comfort. But then, she'd probably already gone to the cliffs.

So, a car accident, a suicide, and now a heart attack. It was a lot of deaths in a row, but the first two seemed... Benign wasn't the word, but they didn't seem like murders. Was Mrs Flyte just the unlucky third in one of those odd strings of sad events that life seems to unleash at times? Like a tragic version of one of those days when you spill coffee down your front, stub your toe and find your computer's crashed and deleted something important, all within a few hours. Mrs Flyte hadn't been the most organised person. You could see that just by walking round the house. Maybe it wasn't *so* far-fetched to imagine she kept aspirin in old prescription bottles. Maybe *she'd* mixed them up when she felt her attack coming on. She'd mixed up Winston's booking, after all. Or so it seemed, at least. No foul play: just an unfortunate accident.

I was comforted by the thought; then the single sneaky word 'but' slithered across my mind, leaving everything behind it shivery and unsettled. *But Nick.* I could believe in an unfortunate car crash, a mind at breaking point pushed to suicide, and a coincidentally timed heart attack – bad things, like good, tended to come in threes. But why, then, had Nick lured me out here and then pretended to know nothing about it. Or, if he hadn't, who had made it look like he had?

'What you don't seem to understand is that we're not safe here!' Bella's voice, loud with fear, cut through my cogitations.

'I understand perfectly. I simply don't see what shouting and gesticulating will do to help.'

Winston's manner was the opposite of Bella's. He sat, reclining by the fire, delicately adjusting a trouser leg to display the correct amount of silk sock, smooth and unruffled in voice and appearance. Although there was the matter of his stubble. Had he not had time to shave this morning? That felt somehow out of character for such a fastidious man. My mind began turning over the question of what he could have been doing, up so early but too busy to shave, out on the cliffs. Before I could form more than the vague outline of a suspicion, Bella stood and let loose a series of panicked profanities, pulling at herself, now her shiny gold locks, now her dress, with wild, darting eyes. Ravi, somewhere between the two in terms of self-control, was trying to calm her, but she pushed away his ministrations.

'We have to do something. Search the house, call the police again, search the island even. We can't just sit here and wait!'

'But we can. Of course, I won't stop you from seizing that axe above the mantel and wandering from room to room in search of a ghost who interfered with our late hostess's medication. But, even with my glancing knowledge of the horror film and the Gothic novel, I can tell you that if this place *is* haunted, going off alone to investigate is a murderously bad idea.'

'What's your suggestion, then? That we just relax by the fire till the police arrive?'

'It strikes me as both safer and more pleasant. I suppose we could pass the time by partaking of a meal at some point.'

'That might not be so easy, actually,' said James, re-entering the room, though I hadn't noticed him leave. 'I've just been looking through the kitchen cupboards, and we're pretty low on supplies.'

'But surely you can make do?' said Winston. 'You've been so resourceful in that department thus far. It would be a pity to ruin your reputation now.'

'I'll do what I can, of course. But perhaps you'd all better come and see. There's plenty of booze, but not much else. If the police don't get us off this island soon, we're going to be very hungry come tomorrow evening. Or very drunk.'

James hadn't been lying about the state of the cupboards. I prodded a single tin of tuna, balanced on its curve, which rolled loudly around an otherwise empty shelf.

'Not even any pasta?' I asked. 'You made such a delicious lunch.'

'Thanks. But no, there's none left. As far as I can tell, we're down to water biscuits, frozen sweetcorn, a badly out-of-date tin of fish paste and this slightly mouldy bread. Plus enough whisky to drown a cow, of course.'

'And this tuna,' I said, flicking it with my finger so it would do another lazy, resonant circle.

'And the tuna. So maybe we're looking at some sort of sweetcorn-tuna-casserole situation?'

'With crushed water biscuits on top for texture. I feel like Audrey Hepburn in *Sabrina*. You know, when she makes a soufflé out of crackers?'

'Prettier, though.'

That silenced me for a minute. I hid my blush by sticking my head into a low cupboard, as though I were trying to be really thorough and check its dark corners. But there was something in there after all.

'What do you think this opens?' I asked, re-emerging and bringing the rather large and rusty old-fashioned key I'd found with me. 'It was just in a corner of the cupboard.'

'Obviously hasn't been used in a while.' James picked some

fluff and cobwebs off it. 'Keep it, maybe you'll find the door it unlocks. Hopefully there'll be some food behind it.'

'Why, are we really that low?' This was Ravi, who came in holding hands with Bella. She seemed a little less twitchy, perhaps distracted by the question of supplies. Winston had announced in the library that he would be having a doze by the fire and we should sort out the food problem without him.

'Oh, so we'll just do everything for you, then,' Bella had objected.

'Babe, just let it go,' Ravi had tried to soothe her. I had wanted to point out that she had yet to do anything for anyone, when I remembered that she had in fact made Ravi a restorative tea. And Mrs Flyte had also drunk it. That was food for thought, so I had stayed quiet and left them bickering, to go and help James make a dispiriting census of the pantry.

Now the pair seemed to have smoothed their ruffled feathers, though I doubted Bella's animosity towards Winston had entirely died down.

'Didn't she, like, keep some stores or something?' Ravi was saying. 'It seems crazy to live out here on your own like this, so isolated, and not have a well-stocked kitchen.'

'I guess she stocked up on the things that mattered to her,' said James, opening the whisky cupboard to display its bounty. 'I mean, at least we can get drunk on New Year's.'

Bella shuddered.

'Getting pissed on whisky in a house that contains a dead body is not what I was picturing when I decided to come to this party.'

'Nor me,' I agreed glumly. 'I was planning on...' But I stopped before mentioning Nick. Somehow, after the phone call we'd had, and after James's comment about Audrey Hepburn, I just didn't want to bring him up. 'I was planning on having a much better time.'

'We can still have a good time!' Ravi's determination to party seemed a bit demented, under the circumstances, but he was more puppyish than debauched, and it was almost endearing. So there was a certain amount of humour in my tone as I asked:

'Literally, how?'

'Well, we could think of it like a wake. You know, drink in honour of the dead, reminisce about the good times they had, that kind of thing.'

Bella snorted.

'What, like the time Mrs Flyte served me a cabbage leaf for dinner?'

'Huh, yeah, or the time at school with Penny, when...' Suddenly the air between them was charged. Ravi looked at the floor. Bella glared at Ravi. James and I glanced at each other from the corners of our eyes.

'What do we actually have to eat, then?' asked Bella.

'Um, not a lot.' James ticked off the sad list on his fingers.

'This woman had no idea of nutrition. And why did you use up all the eggs this morning?'

'Well, I didn't know we were going to be entirely cut off, or that there was so little in the cupboards to begin with, did I?'

James, of all of us, had maintained the most unruffled surface throughout this increasingly trying weekend. He was sort of disturbingly calm and friendly, even in the face of a dead body or a rising storm. But Bella had finally managed to piss him off. In a weird way, I found it reassuring to hear an edge enter his voice.

'It seems like nobody here was at all capable of planning ahead.' There was something schoolmistressy and stiff about her voice when she was angry; the floaty tones and New Age sugar coating disappeared. Underneath, I got the impression, Bella was just a really bossy girl who happened to like tie-dye and astrology.

'Chill out, Bells, we're all in this together. We all thought we'd be catered for, didn't we? It was supposed to be, like, a luxury experience, right?'

She sighed and visibly tried to bring her irritation under control. Ravi was used to handling her, I supposed.

'Some of us still *are* being waited on. Have you noticed how he never lifts a finger? Just gets everyone to do things for him.' She jerked her head back towards the hall, presumably to indicate Winston in the other room, but in a quirk of timing that made me smile, he came walking through the door.

'My dear, you know, I used to have to do things for people. But then eventually I tried it this way round, and it's so much more enjoyable. I decided never to go back. Speaking of which, I can't really settle down to my snooze without a drink first. Would one of you mind? Since our departed hostess is no longer hoarding the supply.'

Winston waggled an empty tumbler at the room and flashed a malicious grin.

How many is that today? I wondered, even as I suppressed a smile at his timing.

Bella hadn't seen the funny side, though. Her beautiful face was snarled up, preparing some righteous refusal, but when she opened her mouth, the sound we all heard was:

Yeooooooooowowowowowow...

At first I thought it was her, so inarticulate with rage that she hadn't been able to form a sentence, though that seemed an outsized reaction. But her face had gone from snarling to bewildered along with the rest of us, and the sound hadn't seemed to come from this room. The hairs on my neck prickled. I huddled into my big woollen pullover and told myself the wind had found a new way to breach the house's walls.

Yauuuuuuuuhuhuhuh...

'You can hear that, right?' whispered Ravi.

We all nodded, obeying some impulse towards silence.

'Do you think Mrs Flyte's woken up?' he asked.

'Unless she's woken up as a zombie,' said James, also in a whisper, 'no.'

'That *would* explain the, ah, alteration in her speaking voice,' said Winston.

'Stop being ridiculous!' Bella's whisper was seething. 'It's obviously not her... It's *them*.'

We were quiet. Bella meant ghosts, and though I'd been laughing at her with the rest of them earlier, that otherworldly wail put a different colour on her theory now.

'Has anyone changed their mind about the whole searching the house idea? Do you still think it's stupid?' We looked at Ravi, looked at each other, and shook our heads. 'Then let's go.'

If my throat hadn't been choking on fear, I might have giggled as we tiptoed in single file down the hall. Ravi, in spite of his weak stomach, led the way. Bella was right behind him, reaching forward to hold his hand. Winston tried to make a show of strolling casually along, but I could see sweat standing out on the back of his neck. When I looked behind me, James half-smiled, but he didn't look like he believed in his own reassurance.

At the bottom of the stairs we paused, hoping for some kind of reprieve. Maybe we would realise it was just a creaky door. But the weird yell came again, obviously from the floor above and unmistakably *alive*. Or, if not alive, at least undead.

Yeeeeaughaughaughaugh…

There was nothing to do but go up. We mounted the stairs so quietly you could hear each creaky tread protest five times as we passed over. At the top we spread out, unsure which direction the sound had come from.

'We should split up,' mouthed James.

'That's a bad idea!' said Ravi.

'Not each on our own. But two groups. You go that way: we'll go this.' He was pulling me along with him, and in spite of my fear I felt a little thrill that he assumed I'd come with him. Winston paused, considering his choices.

'I'll go with these two.' He nodded at Ravi and Bella. 'Any wee ghosties will take them first, I imagine.'

They set off, halting and all trying to keep behind each other, down one branch of the hallway. We turned and began making our way down the other.

At the end of the hallway there was a window, and then it turned to the left. Though a storm was brewing, and the light faded fast in Scotland in December, it was still too early to be dark. I could see clouds hurrying on their way, dark grey skeins unravelling against a paler grey sky. I kept my eyes on that rectangle of faltering light as we moved slowly down the corridor, passing misty mirrors and portraits that seemed to watch us as we passed. It wasn't dark outside, but already the hall lights were necessary in the big gloomy house, and the fitful bulbs, occasionally giving up and then spitting back to life under their blanket of cobwebs, made my heart pound harder – so hard now that, if the scream came again, I wasn't sure I'd hear it over the thudding. *It'll be wind in the eaves*, I told myself. But then I thought of the strange scuttles and slams in the night.

Wham!

A dark blot blocked out most of the window suddenly, and I shrieked and grabbed James's arm. It pulsed and struggled and then resolved into a black corvid, too big to be anything but a raven blown sideways by the wind, trying to sort out its feathers and fly away.

'What is it?!' The others had come running up behind us, evidently believing we'd found the source of the wailing.

'Nothing.' I gave a little breathy, embarrassed laugh. 'A bird hit the window. Did you find anything?'

'No, but –'

Yeaoughuuuuuuuuu…

It was coming from around the bend in the corridor. We moved forward in a bunch, holding our breath as we looked round. But there was nothing to be seen in the hall itself. The first door on the left was Mrs Flyte's, and we paused there, looking at each other, everybody wondering whether we ought to go in, afraid of what we might find, and afraid, too, of what we were certain to find. But then the sound came again, not from behind her door, but from farther along the corridor. I wasn't sure whether to be relieved or even more terrified.

Near the end of the hall was a narrow wooden door with a rusty lock and a round iron handle. The high-pitched, inhuman moan was coming from behind it. We stood there, half-paralysed. Then Winston muttered 'godsake' under his breath and reached out to try the handle. It rattled, but the door wouldn't budge. The wailing came louder now.

'I wonder…' said James. 'Millie, give me that key you found.'

It took me a moment to realise what he was talking about: that thing from the bottom of the cupboard. I took the heavy, old-fashioned key from my pocket and passed it to him. He put it in the lock, and it turned. We looked at each other, I nodded, and, while the rest of us cringed backwards, he slowly pulled the door open, wincing at the shrieking hinges.

It was a broom cupboard, and out from among the tumbled buckets and dried-stiff mops strolled a ginger cat.

CHAPTER 12

'Damn.' The others looked at me. 'There goes our claim to the tuna.'

Winston smiled first, then laughed, letting his belly bob up and down with a freedom he rarely showed. James began to grin, then he was gasping too, and one by one each of us followed until finally we were all bent over in the corridor, hysterical, wiping our eyes and struggling for breath. The cat cocked its head and flicked its tail quizzically.

The laughter faded, and we were left in that disappointed silence that often follows an attack of the giggles. Suddenly Ravi's gaze sharpened and he looked at the rest of us a little uneasily.

'What is it, babe?' said Bella.

'It's just… Who locked it in there? Why do that to a cat?'

Why indeed? It was an action that revealed a mean streak, but whose?

James leaned over and flipped the lock on the inside of the cupboard door. It moved easily in his hand.

'I bet it was an accident. Look, the lock turns at a pretty light touch. If the cat went in there and the door slammed…'

'The house *is* very draughty,' I agreed. The others nodded slowly, seeming half-reassured.

'Let's see if we can find your bowl,' said James to the cat, which trotted off towards the stairs, while we followed behind.

On our way down the hall, I stopped in front of one of the paintings. It was like all the others: a dark oil with a varnishy sheen, which made me question its authenticity. It depicted a chinless denizen of the eighteenth or nineteenth century, a woman with bunches of sausage curls over her ears and everything from her bosom to the column her plump elbow was resting on swathed in tartan. It had neither beauty nor originality, but it had caught my eye. Why? I looked at the one next to it: a man with a gun and a dog and a few dead animals slung over his plaid. Had they been hung the other way round when we first walked this way? Both of their gazes were on me, as though they wanted to see whether I could figure it out. I shivered and walked downstairs.

I turned into the library, worn out by successive fits of fear and laughter, and wanting to collapse in front of the fire. Ravi was there already; the others were moving on into the kitchen, making noises about tea.

'That's a relief, eh?' He smiled at me, pushing back his shiny hair, handsome again now that terror and queasiness weren't sucking the colour from his face.

'Only if you like cats.'

'Don't you?'

'They're cute. But they eat too many birds.'

'Oh, right, that's your thing, isn't it? Birdwatching and that?'

'It is. It used to be my job, even. I worked for a bird protection charity.'

At this, he gave me the kind of wincing smile you offer someone who's just made an embarrassing admission about the state of their bowels. Clearly my career, which had been dear to me and which I was still mourning, didn't register on his scale of success.

'Very noble, I imagine.'

'It's important work, though I suppose you don't find it glamorous. We lobbied and nearly got a key piece of protective legislation passed last year.' The wince turned into more of a smirk when I said the word *nearly*. 'But what do you do, anyway? Something in finance, right?'

'Well, I guess I'm a broker, but I turn my hand to a lot. Once you have a feel for money...' He shrugged complacently. 'There's an art to it.'

'And you're an artist. Huh. That's how you know Winston, right?'

'Ahem... Yes, well, he and I have worked together before, yes, but...' He leaned closer to me and looked over his shoulder towards the door, as though anxious someone might come in. 'I wouldn't normally tell you this, but considering the circumstances... He's not the first person I was hoping to see when I walked in here, if I'm perfectly honest.'

'Oh? Why?'

'Well, nothing serious. Just a bit of confusion over some transactions.' He frowned at me, seeming to weigh me up. Evidently, he wanted to confide in someone, but wasn't sure the risk I represented was worth it. 'Really, it just boils down to the fact that he's a client. You know how it is. You don't want to be thinking about work when you're ready to play.'

I guess I hadn't made the cut.

'Not really an issue in my line of work.'

'Well, no, ha! It wouldn't be. Not if birds are your clients.' He laughed at his own remark and spread his arms out on the back of the sofa.

'The birds weren't actually… Never mind. Oh, hello, Winston.'

Ravi jumped and whipped his head round. If Winston hadn't actually been walking into the room, it would have been worth pretending just for the sight.

'By some judicious scraping of the mouldiest bits of bread, and a thorough exploration of both nooks and crannies, we've cobbled together some tea and toast.'

His hands were full of stacked cups on the left and saucers on the right, which he set down with a clatter while he was speaking – although perhaps orating was a better word for it.

'One of you *could* go through and help the others.'

'I'll go!' Ravi was up like a shot and out of the library door.

Winston and I shared a wry smile.

'He's been telling me about his work for you. Apparently, you're not his happiest client?'

'Ah.' He settled in the very spot that Ravi had just vacated, the sofa corner nearest the fire, and took his time making himself comfortable, smoothing his tie, tidying his trouser legs. 'That boy has been rather naughty with my money, and I have found him out. Do you know, I don't think he was entirely pleased to see me here.'

'You don't mean… Has he actually been stealing from you?'

'More like borrowing with the intention to return, and thinking I would't notice. But I notice everything.' He gave me an over-the-top-of-his-glasses look, though he wasn't wearing any.

'Do you?'

'I do.' Again, there was a kind of emphasis in his voice that had meaning, but I couldn't decipher it. 'For instance… you.'

'Me.'

'You're an interesting girl. Demure, apparently, and agreeable. But with hidden aspects.' He had been inspecting his nails while he said this, then flicked his eyes up to meet mine on the last words. Suddenly I felt as I had done on the cliffs when we found Penny – an insect on a pin, squirming on the point of his gaze. The fire wasn't so warming any more.

'I don't have anything to hide.'

'We all have things we hide. Some of them are perfectly innocent, of course. Some less so.'

'Look, I'm not sure why you're saying this to me, but I can assure you, I'm as bewildered as anyone here by what's going on.'

'Are you? I wonder.'

Those eyes, wide and keen as a cat's, narrowed down on me. I wished I'd sounded more confident, more affronted. More innocent.

'And what about you?' I tried to reverse the accusation. 'You seem pretty sure of everything.'

'A professional stance, merely,' he replied with a dismissive hand gesture. 'I've learned to project certainty. It spares people like me a certain amount of effort when we're constantly being challenged.'

'People like you, meaning lawyers?'

'Lawyers, yes. But also black men. Or the gay sons of fervently religious immigrants to a godless nation. Take your pick.'

This was chastening. Whatever he asked me now, I felt I owed him a straight answer.

'So what, specifically, have you been wondering?'

He smiled and thought about it for a moment. Then he raised a hand with the index and middle fingers held up in a V for victory.

'Two things. First, I've been wondering where you found that terribly convenient key.'

'The one that opened the broom cupboard? It was in the kitchen, just lying at the back of a shelf. I found it when James and I were taking stock of our supplies.'

'Ah. And it was you who found it, was it?'

I was quiet for a moment, looking at him, trying to assess the implications of his line of questioning.

'Are you trying to highlight the fact that James was there? Just as he was there in Mrs Flyte's room, to find her, and to notice the pills in the medicine bottle were wrong? Because it was me who found the key that let the cat out. And it was me who found the medicine bottle first.'

'Just so. It was you.'

I had been trying to protect James. A somewhat perverse instinct. After all, I had been suspicious of his involvement with the pills. Who better than a pharmacist to meddle with someone's medication? But now it appeared that I was condemning myself in Winston's eyes. I shifted uncomfortably in my sagging armchair and looked away from him, out of the window. It was nearly dark. I hoped they'd be along with the tea soon.

'I had a second query, you may remember.'

'Oh, yes. Fire away.'

'That phone call you made a short time ago – it didn't seem to make you very happy. Who was on the end of the line?'

Now I was really evading his gaze. I could see what he was doing, in his meticulous, unhurried, lawyerly way: building a case against me. Neither of us, probably, was even sure that there was a case to build against anybody. But if there was, Winston was getting out ahead of it and making sure he could point the finger elsewhere. I knew this, and I didn't want to be his scapegoat. But I also didn't want to explain about Nick and my gullibility about the invitation. Eager to avoid either implicating or embarrassing myself, I aimed for a neutral reply.

'A former colleague.'

'Indeed. From your Flights days? Interesting, isn't it, how your former colleagues keep popping up this weekend? Popping up and then popping their clogs. I hope this one made it to the end of the conversation alive?'

So much for neutrality. Fortunately, at this point the others walked in, Ravi carrying a high pile of golden toast and James and Bella each armed with a fat-bellied brown teapot. I snatched at the toast. The hot buttery taste was comforting. Then I poured a cup of tea and stood up, gulping at it as I made for the door.

'You know, I could really use some fresh air, and if I don't go now it'll be too dark and wet. I'll see you all in a bit.'

They nodded me out of the room. As I looked back, I saw that Ravi's attention was on the food; Bella was looking sceptically out of the window at the rainy twilight; James's interest drifted to the others, as did his easy smile. But Winston's eyes narrowed, and he didn't look away from me as I left. His gaze, sharp as the axe over the fireplace, followed me over the rim of his cup.

I put my dirty china in the sink and left the house by the kitchen door. Hanging next to Winston's long overcoat on the rack above the umbrella stand was a slouchy old green jacket. It must have belonged to Mrs Flyte. I shrugged myself into it, feeling a bit strange about wearing a dead woman's clothes, but too impatient to go upstairs for my own coat. I considered the umbrellas – and the shotgun – in the stand. But it was already blowing strong out there, so there didn't seem much point.

As I stepped out of the door and the wind filled my ears, I realised I had been hearing it all along. It was louder now, of course, but was still audible all the time within the house.

It rose and fell from howl to whine, buffeting the windows and pulling at the eaves, a constant reminder of the fragility of even that enormous shelter. A background complaint against our presence, sitting habitually just outside consciousness.

But now I was conscious of it, and not just of its noise. The gale nearly flattened me. I considered turning back; I was bent double trying to make headway against the wind, and the icy rain was stinging my face and knifing its way through my clothes. But I hadn't been lying – I needed fresh air and solitude, a break from the heavy atmosphere building inside the house. I didn't feel free, though, in spite of the empty hills and strong wind. The atmosphere had followed me, or perhaps it belonged to the island, a resentful rock hoping to shake us off its back.

I pulled the jacket tighter around me. It was too big to have been Mrs Flyte's originally, I decided. It must have belonged to the husband who'd owned the house. I turned my back to the wind. The growing storm was too strong for me to head towards the cliffs, as I'd planned, but if I went around the house to where the outbuildings were, I'd probably find some shelter and some privacy.

I hunkered down in the lee of one of the sheds. I couldn't see the house, or much of anything really. I was staring at another shed's blank wall. If the weather had been calmer, it might have been worth scanning the sky for birds. That would have settled me, smoothed my own ruffled feathers. Twilight was a good time, with some settling into their nests, some grabbing a last mouthful of insects, and some night fliers beginning to stir and make themselves known. But in these conditions every creature was hunkering down, protecting itself from the elements. Except me.

Why? Why was I out in the cold and the storm, rather than sat by the fire in the library? *Because I don't feel safe in that house*, said a frightened and frightening voice in my head. That was the bare fact. I didn't understand what was happening, but I knew it scared me.

My mind kept turning over the pieces of the situation, trying to make them fit. They didn't. I couldn't see why Nick had invited me here and then pretended not to know about it, or how anyone could have faked that. I couldn't understand why two accidental deaths and a suicide had been followed by something that looked more purposeful. And I couldn't imagine who had locked a cat in the broom cupboard. But these things had happened. And even though I couldn't find any rational explanation for them, my instincts told me they pointed to danger.

Not just any danger, though, said some more honest part of myself. *You suspect someone.* It was true. The way he'd found Penny, and so visibly enjoyed seeing the rest of us find her too; the way he'd lied about drinking alone; the way he seemed to be trying to trap me into something – Winston scared me. I didn't trust his actions or his intentions.

But still the kaleidoscope turned, refusing to settle into a clear pattern. Bella was prickly, too; Ravi obviously had a loose relationship to the law; James was cagey and changeable and had come here to supply drugs to the party. And what about Mrs Flyte's peculiar reticence about how the booking had been made? And that sudden nastiness she had displayed before lunch? Her death would seem to put her beyond suspicion, but it still made me uneasy, the way she'd reacted when I questioned her. Had she been trying to hide something, for herself or someone else? Something for which she'd been killed, to keep it a secret? Then there was the house, with its unplaceable creaks, doors that drifted open, paintings that changed place and watched you from the walls. Ghosts?

I leaned my head back against the wall and squeezed my eyes shut. The wind howled above me; the rain had soaked my hair and was now trickling down my neck. My hands were so cold I couldn't grip them, the fingers locked in stiff open claws that I tried to chafe back into mobility. The storm-soaked ground was seeping through my trousers where I was crouched. But worse than the cold and the wet was the sick fright in my heart and my stomach, the dark things lurking in unexamined corners of my mind. I wished with every part of my chilled and shivering self that when I opened my eyes, things would be different.

Crunch, crunch, crunch.

Someone was walking along the gravel path around the buildings. Someone in search of me? Whoever it was, I didn't want to be found. I held my breath and hoped. At least this wish came true: the steps passed behind the shed that was sheltering me and out of earshot. But if they had come looking for me, I had better go back to the house. I sighed and braced myself for the windy walk back to the front door.

When I came in, the relative warmth of the house was welcome. I stood wringing out my hair on the hall rug, steaming gently and reluctant to join the others.

But then I realised I wasn't alone. Bella was standing at the top of the stairs. She was completely quiet and completely still, which was why I hadn't noticed her. Her hair was almost as wet as mine. It, too, was dripping onto the floor around her feet. But it wasn't wet with water.

It was wet with blood.

CHAPTER 13

I stood by the door, staring at Bella, and she stood on the landing, staring at me. Across the expanse of the hall, the tiny, twinned drips coming from our hair punctuated the silence. Slowly her breathing began to grow louder, until I couldn't hear her hair dripping blood or mine dripping water, only the rough and rapid noise of her hyperventilating. Soon, I thought, she would probably scream.

But before she could, Winston emerged from the library. He was yawning and stretching, a cat waking from its nap. He saw me first, frozen by the door.

'Was it worth it going out in that? You look half-dead.'

I whimpered a little at this choice of words. I still couldn't speak. Then his eyes finally followed my gaze, across the flagstones and up the stairs. To Bella.

'My God…' he said.

It was the first time since Winston had found Penny that

I'd seen him so unsure of himself. He stood as still as I did, his eyes wide and mouth open.

I began to worry that the three of us would remain fixed in our positions indefinitely. Perhaps James would come along and also be shocked stone-still, and the police would arrive in their boat, days from now, to find the four of us still holding our positions.

The four of us. Four. Because where was…

'Ravi.' Finally Bella had unfrozen. She spoke his name again, with a break in her voice: 'Ravi.' Then she collapsed.

I rushed up the stairs towards her. I couldn't understand. Here was a woman covered in blood, speaking the name of her lover. The implications were obvious, and yet I was rushing towards the danger, not away.

At the top of the stairs, I bent and gathered her into my arms. Again, I surprised myself. I'd spent most of this trip alternately thinking how irritating Bella was and envying her. But now instinct led me to this embrace. She turned and buried her head in my stomach and let out an awful cry. I felt blood seeping from her hair into my pullover and onto my skin.

At this point James did come along, from the passage leading to the kitchen. He was shocked stone-still, as I'd imagined. But only for a moment. Soon, he, too, was rushing up the stairs, and then Winston remembered how to move, and we were all gathered in a knot around Bella.

'Where's Ravi?' asked James.

Bella was still emitting hoarse screams into my muffling torso, but she waved a hand vaguely in the direction of their room, and James went off to find… I didn't want to think what he might find.

Bella withdrew from me suddenly, scrambling back and clinging to the banister. A tremor had begun coursing through her body. Her eyes were huge and round, and they darted between me and Winston. Everything about her bespoke terror and suspicion. But then, she was the one covered in blood.

James's step came back down the hall, slowly, reluctantly. I looked up at him and there was something awful in his face.

'He's dead, isn't he?' said Bella.

James nodded.

'There's… I can't describe it. Millie, Winston, you ought to go and see. I know it's horrible,' he continued, putting up a hand to stay any objection. 'But we all need to have seen the same thing, so we can all talk to the police.'

'You're right,' said Winston. 'Come on, Millie.'

I rose and followed him down the corridor. I looked back and saw James kneeling, reaching out to Bella. But she wasn't looking at him. She was following us with her eyes.

Their door was ajar. 'The Crimson Room', the brass plate read, but I could have guessed: everything from the bloodshot wallpaper to the velvet curtains was in shades of vivid red. The bed was unmade, and Ravi and Bella's huge suitcases lay open here and there around the room, spilling their contents onto carpets and footstools.

I could hear the fan running in the bathroom. The door was pulled to, but a crack of light showed around the door.

Winston and I looked at each other. We began to pick our way around the tumbled clothes across the floor. At the bathroom door we paused. I took a breath and nodded at Winston, and he pressed the door gently with his finger. It drifted open.

The fittings in here were plain white, not scarlet, but nonetheless the theme continued. Horribly. Blood covered the floor in a dark sticky film; it streaked the mirror and had soaked through a towel that had fallen from the rail. And the source of all this blood was Ravi.

He was slumped against the corner of the bath, leaning back on the wall. I could see his phone, face up in the blood on the floor; it explained what he had come here for. The screen was frozen on an image of a woman with pneumatic breasts beginning to unbutton her top. His trousers weren't open, he had at least been spared that indignity.

But my attention was fleeing to these details because I couldn't bear to look at the main thing. I forced my eyes upward. I forced myself to see.

The blood had mostly flowed from the six-inch gash at the base of Ravi's neck. It cut into his shoulder, and I could see a white flash of shattered collarbone. The wound had probably been made by an axe. Probably the same axe that was now embedded in his skull.

Winston made a small *tsk* with his tongue and teeth.

'And he was such a handsome boy.'

One half of his face still was: the glossy dark hair tumbling over the brow, the heavily lashed eye, the full mouth and strong jaw. But the other half? The axe from the library mantelpiece had been driven down through it. There was no question that James had been right. He was dead.

In the hall, going back to join the others, Winston held me back a moment, grabbing me by the arm.

'Did you see that on the mirror?'

'The blood?'

'I thought it said something.'

'I didn't notice… I mean I was mostly looking at… you know.'

He nodded slowly, but didn't let me go or start moving again.

'You realise what's going to happen now?'

'When the police arrive, you mean?'

'Well before that, my pet.'

I looked at him blankly.

'There are four people here living. And one person dead. Well, two. Or three if that poor girl's still at the bottom of the cliff. We're on a tiny island. No one's come on or off since we arrived.'

'Which means whoever did that to Ravi –'

'Is still here. It could be you.'

'Or you.'

'Or me. Or the young man's sweetheart. Or *your* prospective sweetheart.' I flinched a little at that. I'd barely even allowed myself to think along those lines. To have Winston articulate my own half-formed romantic wish, moments after we'd been staring at a mutilated body, wasn't even slightly how I wanted to acknowledge my feelings for the first time. 'It could be any of us, and it definitely is one of us.'

'So, until the police arrive…'

'We're going to have to watch each other very carefully indeed.'

I couldn't tell what lay behind this warning. It seemed friendly enough – which was odd in itself, given the sparkling malice that characterised Winston's whole approach to life – but, remembering how he'd questioned me before I went for my walk, I wondered if there was more significance to it than I could see.

Before I went on that walk… It seemed a lifetime ago now, though I supposed it was only three quarters of an hour.

At the top of the stairs, James was encouraging Bella to stand. She seemed listless and unresponsive, but as we approached and her gaze focused on us, she struggled to her feet. Slowly she raised a finger to point in our direction and, in a voice hoarse from weeping, said:

'You did this, didn't you?'

We stopped.

'You fucking killed him. You killed him…'

She broke down again and buried her face in her blood-stained hands.

'I can assure you, I did not kill him,' said Winston, convincingly outraged.

She raised her head and looked searchingly at him, then turned her hard gaze on me.

'*I* didn't do it! Obviously I didn't, I was out of the house the whole time.'

'Well… We don't know that,' said Winston.

'You *do* know that! And why are you trying to point the

finger at me? You're the one who had a reason to want him dead.'

'A reason? You mean the money? Don't be ridiculous. That's not the kind of thing –'

'Quiet!' James's voice cut across mine and Winston's, and we fell silent. Bella gulped back more sobs. 'This isn't how we're going to figure out what happened. Look, if we turn on each other… it just won't work. We're all in shock. Let's go down to the kitchen and make some strong tea, and then we'll each explain to the others where we were and what we were doing for the past hour.'

We exchanged a four-way glance, and everybody gave a curt nod or shrugged their assent. We filed down the stairs, silent. I looked back and saw that we had all left bloody footprints behind us, which were getting paler and paler with each step.

CHAPTER 14

In the kitchen we each leaned against separate surfaces, quiet and wary. The only sounds were the kettle boiling and the wind battering the house. I smelled of blood. Bella's hair had stained the front of my pullover.

The kettle clicked off and we all watched James make the world's most deliberate pot of tea. Four bags went in: one, two, three, four. He stirred. Four cups came out of the cupboard, making four separate china *chinks* on the side. When he got out the sugar, Bella began to object, but he silenced her.

'For shock. It's customary. But I'm glad to see you can think about healthy eating again. You must be coming back to yourself.'

A tiny corner of my mouth wanted to twitch into a smile. But then Ravi flashed through my mind again, bloodied and broken open. The smile died.

Finally, all the tea was poured and milked and sugared, and we were sipping and looking at each other warily.

'I can start,' said James, breaking the silence, which had begun to thicken. 'It's relatively simple. I came back here to clear up the tea and toast things, and when I came back out I found you... at the top of the stairs,' he finished euphemistically.

'And what time was this?' asked Winston.

'I don't know. I don't obsessively check the time.'

'Nonetheless, we ought to try to establish it, roughly. The police will be wanting a coherent narrative when they arrive.'

'Let them establish it, then,' I said, feeling defensive of James. 'Shouldn't we leave it to the professionals?'

'But I *am* a professional.'

'I can try to guess.' James screwed up his face to indicate hard thinking. 'I did see the time when we were making tea. That was around three o'clock. And what is it now?'

We all swivelled our heads towards the clock over the doorway, which stood at just past twenty to five.

'Right, so we had some tea, and Millie left pretty quickly, and then after a while I came back in here to clean everything up. Maybe that was quarter to four? I didn't hurry about washing up, and then I stayed here browsing the cookbooks for a while, torturing myself really, since the cupboards are bare. Then I heard the door open – the front door – so I figured Millie was back, and I thought I'd come and see what everyone was up to. That was, I don't know, fifteen minutes ago?' He looked at Winston, shrugging as though to apologise for the inexactness of his calculations.

Winston nodded and worked his fingers, calculating.

'Very well, let's accept that you were out of sight for… perhaps thirty-five minutes, starting from ten to four. Until that point you were with the rest of us in the library. Well, not all of the rest of us.' He looked at me, expectant; I hoped not accusatory.

'I don't know when I left. I don't know how long I was outside. I don't know anything. I don't understand why any of this is happening!'

I had started speaking calmly, but as the sentences followed each other a catch built in my voice and then I was nearly crying. I set my tea down and covered my face. After a moment I felt a hand on my shoulder and looked up to see James giving me a sympathetic grimace.

'Just try, Millie, I know it's horrible.'

Behind him, Winston and Bella were looking at me with harder eyes. I gulped and tried to shake the weakness out of my voice.

'I left to get some fresh air, to try and think through what's happening here.'

'I thought you left because I was questioning you too closely,' said Winston, looking down at his tea while he spoke.

'Do you want to hear my sequence of events or not?' He nodded, giving way. 'I don't know exactly when I went out. The tea had arrived in the library, so I suppose it was maybe quarter past three? I walked around a little, but the storm…'

We all listened to it for a moment, remembering for the first time since – well, remembering for the first time in a little while, anyway, that it was there, blowing and raining and battering the house. I clutched my hot mug a little closer.

'So I went around to where there are those sheds and things, and I found a spot out of the wind. I didn't think I was gone for very long. But I was thinking. You can't deny we've had a lot to think about. Maybe I was lost in thought for longer than I realised.'

'And how long was it between your coming in and my emerging from the library?'

I tried to think, but my mind shied away from that moment. The horror of seeing Bella, dripping blood at the top of the stairs – it seemed as if the time in which I had stood there, facing her, was infinite, as if the moment had never ended. I shook my head.

'I don't have a clue, really. It could have been seconds or minutes. I just don't know.'

'It was a few minutes before James re-emerged from the kitchen, at any rate. So let us suppose you were back no earlier than a quarter past four. Meaning you were out of sight of any of us for approximately an hour.'

'I'm not sure I like what your phrasing implies, but, yes, I guess the timeline is probably about right.'

He looked at Bella next. The blood had dried in her hair by now, and the darkened locks moved stiffly as she shook her head. It made me feel sick.

'Oh no, I'm not explaining where I've been until you explain where you've been.'

'You speak as though you have some special reason to suspect me.'

'Don't I?' She jutted her neat chin out defiantly.

Winston looked at me and James, his hands to his chest and his eyes wide in innocent protest. I looked down, thinking of what he'd told me about Ravi's indiscretion with his money.

'If you insist, then. Though I think I have the least to defend of any of us here. I drank my tea and ate my toast like a good boy after Millie bolted. Then I began to feel sleepy. You'll recall that my attempts to rest my eyes this afternoon were interrupted by that yowling cat. Where is the cat, by the way?'

Bella waved this question away impatiently, unwilling to be diverted.

'As I was saying, I began to feel sleepy. I don't remember the rest of you leaving the room. I slipped into sweet oblivion and thence into a rather delightful dream about a nude bathing party I once held by a river one hot summer long ago.'

'Wait,' I stopped him. 'You were napping in the library?'

'Yes.'

'On the sofa by the fire?'

'No better place, surely?'

'By the fire, above which the axe was hanging.'

'Ah.' For a moment even cool, collected Winston seemed ruffled. 'I can assure you that it wasn't me who took it down.'

Bella snorted.

'Thanks for the reassurance.'

'You're most welcome. Where was I? Oh yes, on the banks of the Isis, wearing only a spray of leaves. Then I woke up. I imagine it was the door closing which woke me. The time, which I checked on waking, was a quarter past four. And you've had me in sight since then.'

'So you don't know how long you were alone for?' I asked.

'I do not. *She* will have to answer that question.'

We all looked at Bella. She opened her mouth, but then a shudder ran through her body and she buried her face in her hands.

'There, now.' James had crossed to her and was stroking her back in smooth circles while she sobbed. 'Let's sit you down. Maybe some of that whisky, Millie? Much better than tea, silly of me not to think of it.'

I brought her the whisky and a glass, and we waited a little for the grief and horror to stop convulsing her body. Winston, however, was impatient.

'It's a terrible thing that's happened, but you're not off the hook for an explanation. The rest of us have showed our hands; it's your turn now, my dear.'

'I'm not your dear! Not when you're the one –'

'Don't bandy about accusations. Leave that to the police. Until they arrive, we are all stuck here, and one of us is dangerous, so let's refrain from stirring the situation up, shall we?'

Had I been asked to predict how I might react to witnessing a violent murder – or at least its aftermath – and then being told to calm down and answer some questions by the likeliest suspect, I wouldn't have said that I'd take it calmly. And yet, there was such confidence in Winston's directing of the situation, such self-righteous insistence in his manner, as though he knew exactly how such a thing should be handled. Or as though he had imagined handling it in advance.

Insane though it seemed, we all meekly acquiesced in his suggestion. Even Bella.

'You fell asleep,' she finally began, after a few ragged breaths and a long glare at him. 'James had already come back through here with the tray. Ravi and I went upstairs. We just wanted to be alone, to talk, to think about what was going on. I was going to meditate, maybe find some peace of mind.'

She paused here to give a little bitter laugh. I twisted my mouth in acknowledgement of the irony.

'I couldn't settle down and we were bickering a little because he kept telling me to chill. The last thing I said to him was huffy…' Here she briefly covered her face with her hands again. 'He was telling me to "go twiddle a crystal or something", and I kind of stormed out of the room.'

I looked at Winston, then at James. This was quite the admission. It seemed honest and above-board, and surely if she'd killed her boyfriend, she wouldn't admit to having argued with him right before he died? But then it could be a kind of double bluff.

Bella took another of her pained preparatory breaths and carried on with her story.

'So, I just walked down the hall. You know there's that big window at the end that looks out over the sea. I sat down on the chair for a few minutes and watched the waves coming in. Then, when I had calmed down, I went back to make it up with him. At first, I didn't notice anything was wrong. The bathroom light was on and everything was quiet. I thought he was just, you know, in there. I saw the door wasn't fully closed, so I figured he was just sulking. I called his name a couple of times, and, when he didn't answer, I opened the door and…' She broke down again.

'That's all right, we know what you saw,' said James, pouring her another tot of whisky.

'I'm afraid we don't,' said Winston. His arms were crossed over his chest, and he was giving Bella a hard look. 'You were the first to find him, right?'

She nodded assent.

'So, each of us who saw him after only saw what you left behind.'

'What the hell are you implying?'

'I'm not implying anything. I'm stating facts. Another fact is that the rest of us seemed able to enter the room and see what was there without covering ourselves in blood. So why are you soaked from head to toe?'

All at once she was across the kitchen, one of those blood-soaked fingers thrusting into Winston's face.

'Because I got down on the floor with him and took him in my arms, didn't I? Because I loved him. So just get… off… my… back.'

Winston leaned back and smiled.

'Very well. Your affront is noted. Could I just stay on your back a tiny bit longer, though? We still have to clear up the question of time.'

The fight went out of her. She sighed and went to sit at the table.

'When did you and Ravi leave me in the library?' asked Winston.

'Just after James went to clear up. I suppose it must have been ten to four.'

'And you argued as soon as you got into the room?'

'Pretty much. I went to sit in the hall at maybe four o'clock.'

'And went back?'

'I didn't have a watch or anything. It was a few minutes. Ten, maybe? Not much longer than that.'

'So, Ravi was killed between four o'clock and quarter past.'

She nodded. I cleared my throat and voiced the silent implication.

'When none of us had eyes on each other.'

'Indeed.' Winston nodded slowly, his gaze abstracted, as though turning over the possibilities in his mind.

'So, if any of us *could* have done it…' James started but was reluctant to finish.

Once again, I stepped in to complete the thought.

'The question is: which of us *would* have.'

'It's not even a question,' said Bella, still slumped on her chair but eyes lively with rancour and locked on Winston. 'Only *you* had a reason.'

'I see you're unwilling to take my advice about accusations. But I protest. The tiny molehill of financial irregularity that had marred our working relationship is insignificant compared to the mountain of reasons for murder that build up between a couple.'

'There was nothing like that! We're happy. We *were* happy.'

'Happy, maybe, but entirely free of resentment? You're lying to yourself if you're not lying to us. And anyway, you're forgetting that Ravi was not the first person to die on this inhospitable island.'

This struck us all rather forcefully. The gory drama of Ravi's death had put the others out of my mind, but now, in the light of a blatant murder, things looked different.

'You think the girl who jumped – that she might have been pushed?'

I looked closely at Winston as James asked this question. He had been the one to find her, the one to lead us to her, the one to take pleasure in our distress on that clifftop. If anyone had pushed her, it would have been him.

'I saw her jump. There was no one else. But if not pushed physically, perhaps pushed mentally.' I stirred uncomfortably at this. 'And she wasn't the first to die, was she?'

Bella and James looked a little perplexed. Obviously, they had forgotten about the Strangs, which implied they really weren't linked. The suspicions of Nick that had lingered in my mind after our phone call had almost been dispersed by Ravi's murder. But now I could see that three of the deaths over the past few days were linked to Flights, as was Winston, the Strangs' sometime lawyer.

'The couple who died on the mainland. The car crash. But you knew them, too,' I pointed out to Winston.

'As did you.'

'I did, but I didn't take a walk on the cliff at the same time Penny jumped, or fall asleep in the room with the axe that killed Ravi.'

'And I didn't spend years in intimate proximity to the dead man,' parried Winston, with a look at Bella.

I reflected on this, and something else came back to me.

'You were at school with Penny, too, weren't you? Both you and Ravi.'

Bella gave a minimal nod, not looking at me, picking at the ends of her bloodied hair.

'But you...' I turned to James. 'You didn't know any of us before, did you?'

'Not a one.' The smile he gave was doubtless meant to reassure, but it was toothy and uncertain. He looked like a frightened dog about to bite. And it was strange, too, that in a group of people with so many connections weaving in and out of their pasts, he stood apart, unknown to any of us. The only person I knew for sure was here for dishonest reasons.

'But how did you get invited? Who came looking for your particular skill set?' I pressed him.

'These arrangements – they aren't made using real names. The messages could have come from anyone. Any of you.'

'One last question.' Winston had resumed control of the conversation and was looking piercingly at Bella.

'No, please. I'm covered in blood; I need to shower. And Ravi's dead. Can't you leave me alone?' Her voice was broken and desperate, and, as she spoke, she pulled at her clothes, now stiff with dried blood.

'Just let her clean up,' said James. 'We can always go over it again later.'

Winston shrugged and gestured at the door. Bella got up and began walking out. In the doorframe, though, she paused and looked back.

'My bathroom...'

'I'll get you set up in mine. I promise I haven't made too much of a mess of things.' James, ever helpful, hurried away after her.

I stayed behind, exchanging an ambivalent look with Winston. We were measuring what Bella had said, partly, but we were also measuring each other.

'I have another question for you,' I said finally.

'I had one of those, for Bella. But too late now. Ask away.' He closed his eyes. When he wasn't staring penetratingly at me, his face looked a little tired.

'Who were you drinking with last night, in the library?' Those two sticky glasses that Mrs Flyte had complained about were still bothering me, in spite of all that had happened since.

'Ah. I wanted to be discreet about this earlier, but in light of subsequent events, it's unimportant. I was drinking with your friend, the one who threw herself off the cliff. Was it only this morning?' He pinched the bridge of his nose.

After the last hour, I was surprised to find that I could still be shocked. But I hadn't expected his answer at all. There were implications for his guilt, but it was difficult to think them through while struggling to imagine the two of them, so unalike, sitting up late and having a chat.

'With *Penny*? What did you talk about? Did she give any sign of…'

'Not of that, no. But she did say something interesting to me. About you, as it happens.'

'Oh?'

'That you seemed so nice.'

'Is that interesting?'

'It was the way she said it. There was a particular emphasis on the word "seemed".'

I felt cold. Winston's constant questioning began to make a horrible kind of sense. He'd had a reason to be suspicious of me – a small one, maybe, but a significant one. But I wasn't the only person here he'd cross-examined, nor was I the closest to the murder.

'What was *your* last question? For Bella?'

'Ah, it was a good one.' He smiled to himself, taking a moment to appreciate his own intellect, and I had to prompt him again before he would share it. 'I wanted to ask her how someone got into her room and killed that poor boy without her hearing or, more pertinently, seeing anything.'

'She said she was sat at the end of the hall.'

'Yes, the end with the seat by the window, looking out over the sea. Which is indeed at the end of the hall, just where it turns. And their bedroom comes after the turn. Meaning anyone coming up the stairs to kill Ravi would have had to walk past her to get to the door.'

So, she was lying. But so was everybody else. I remembered the sound of feet crunching past me on the gravel outside. Someone else had been outside, but nobody had admitted it. Then again, no one, including myself, had been perfectly honest during this trip. And my life might depend on figuring out whose lies mattered.

CHAPTER 15

Winston and I were left alone in the kitchen. Feeling awkward – he might be a murderer, after all – I cast about for something to say, and it occurred to me that there was a matter of practical importance to take care of.

'Has anyone called the police yet, to tell them about…'

Winston gave a *tsk* of acknowledgement.

'A good point. You have an organised mind, don't you?'

'More organised than my flat, anyway.'

'Well, why don't you go and call and give them a nice tidy account of what's happened, then.'

But when I settled onto the stool in the little nook, gathered my thoughts to explain this latest death, as far as I could, and lifted the receiver to make the call – the line was dead. I toggled the prongs of the cradle with increasing desperation. No dial tone. Flat silence.

Right. So now I was trapped on an island with three

living strangers, two dead ones, and a friend whose death had looked like suicide but seemed likelier by the minute to have been murder. There was no food – no decent food, anyway – and the only line of communication to the outside world had been cut off. I wouldn't say things were looking up.

'The line's gone dead,' I told Winston on returning to the kitchen.

'That is both inconvenient and interesting. Did you cut it?'

I had become more accustomed to his blunt way of asking questions with damning implications, and I didn't display any of the indignation I would have done a day ago.

'No. Did you?'

'No. One of the others, then.'

'Or the storm?'

'Your willingness to extend us all the benefit of the doubt in the face of escalating violence charms me.'

'I guess I'm just hoping some of this can be explained by bad luck, rather than ill will.'

'It would be very unlucky indeed for an axe to fall off a wall in one room and get stuck in somebody's head in another. But we do seem to have been unfortunate in our hostess, and in her standard of household management. That expired fish paste is beginning to seem more appetising.'

James came in, asking, 'Do either of you happen to know where clean towels might be kept? Mine is wet, and Bella's…'

I could vividly picture just what was wrong with Bella's.

'Bad news. The phone's dead. I tried to contact the police to tell them. But we're cut off.'

'The storm?'

'Another optimist,' said Winston.

'Shit.' James scrubbed his face with his broad hand, but it looked no less sad and tired after. 'Well, at least they already knew to come out here. I'm sure they'll set off once the storm dies down.'

We listened for a moment to the howl of the wind and the rain spatter, and I wondered if that would be soon enough.

'Mrs Flyte's office – she went in there to get our keys. Maybe there are towels and things there,' I suggested.

I went off to investigate, leaving James and Winston in the kitchen. I wasn't sure why it should be me, except that it was woman's work, I guess. No doubt they would be having one of the same blunt, suspicious conversations that Winston seemed to instigate at every turn. Doing a chore – even if it was an errand for Bella – at least gave me a rest from fending off his damning questions.

The office was as shabby as the rest of the place but somehow more welcoming. It was obviously one of the few rooms in frequent use, its clutter human and comfortable rather than abandoned and sad. I could see the keys hanging on a row of hooks over a wooden grid of pigeonholes, now empty of letters, each square framing mere dust or some forgotten object long ago placed there for convenience. The desk was a mass of dark wood, overlooked by a lamp with a green glass shade and a brass chain, which I pulled.

The surface of the desk was a jumble of papers and office miscellany: paper clips, rubber bands, dried-out glue sticks and capless pens. I found traces, too, of the woman she'd been. The same wash of sedimented leaflets that in my flat was composed of RSPB newsletters and WWF donation forms was here formed of bulletins from a home for stray cats and pictures of smiling children, fully recovered from harelip surgery. I felt an odd twinge. She'd seemed dithery and unimpressive to me, but in some small way the world would be a harder place without her, if only for one abandoned feline.

That reminded me of the ginger tom we'd let out of the broom cupboard. As if in response to my thought, something stirred by my feet, and the creature himself leaped up from where he'd been curled underneath the desk. He knocked a pile of folders from their precarious balance, and, as he settled in for a thorough wash, I picked up the papers that had spilled out. I scanned the first one and caught my breath.

They were profiles. Of the guests. All of us.

I rifled through the papers, too quickly to gather specifics, but seeing on each page some fact from one of our lives: 'Ravi Gopal, account manager at AC Investments', 'Winston Harriot, 56, unmarried', 'Millicent Partridge, father deceased'. A school photo of a curly-haired child that might have been Penny. When I came to the page on Bella, I nearly shouted with laughter: her surname was Badcock. No wonder she went by 'Bella B' online.

That embarrassing discovery aside, the files were mostly innocuous, full of the kind of thing you could learn from relatively basic online digging. But not the kind of information that was normal for a hotelier to gather about their guests.

The dossiers were random, badly organised, a jumble of background data, the purpose of which wasn't clear to me.

But they made one thing obvious. We were here for a reason. We had been selected. Targeted. Had we been chosen to die?

I wanted to figure out exactly what I had found, but the thought of Bella, covered in blood and desperate for a shower, was tugging me away. I decided to find her a towel and then come back to the papers for a closer look.

Obviously, there were no supplies in this room. They must be in a cupboard somewhere, perhaps upstairs with the bedrooms. I thought about the helpful brass tag attached to my room key and crossed my fingers. Sure enough, a tarnished oval labelled 'Linen' was hanging at the end of the row. I grabbed it, and then, on impulse, also took the key to the Heather Room, the room Penny had been staying in.

The linen cupboard was a sad affair, which I might have guessed from the state of my own towel. Everything fraying at the edges and line-dried into harsh stiffness. But it was all clean, and that was what Bella needed at the moment. I grabbed a stack of towels, figuring she'd need a few, and headed around the corner to James's room, where she was waiting to wash off the traces of the man she'd loved.

James, fittingly for the only Scot among us, was in the Tartan Room. My brain at first refused to compute. The clash of colours, lines and checks was so extreme that I felt as if I was having a mild stroke. I took a moment to wonder what theme Winston's bedroom delighted in, what aesthetic assault he had to fend off at night in order to sleep. I could picture him – perhaps because of the pale glint of his close-cropped hair – swathed in a slippery silver coverlet, with silver satin drapes on the windows and a lot of mercury glass objects casting confusing reflections from every surface. Whatever the colour, he would have made sure he was given a thoroughly luxurious – even if God-awful – room.

For the moment, though, I was in this migraine-inducing plaid-scape. Bella, in spite of being covered in blood, was a rest for the eyes, slumped on the arm of a blue, green and orange chair.

'I brought you some towels.'

'Right. Thanks.'

She didn't move, just sat staring at her hands.

'I'm sorry.'

'What for?' She raised her eyes to me in mild confusion.

'For...'

'Oh. Thanks.' She slumped again and then suddenly snapped to attention. 'You aren't trying to tell me –'

'That I did it? No. Jesus.' I tossed the towels onto the bed in a huff, ready to leave the room. But the sight of her stopped me – forlorn, not accusatory. Just lost and bewildered. I sat next to the towels and began to apologetically remake the neat stack. 'I never even met you, or Ravi, before yesterday.'

'I know. You're right. It's obvious.'

'You mean...'

'Winston. Who else had a reason to do it?' She looked at me searchingly. She was really asking. I took a breath and decided to tell the truth.

'Well, we're all wondering if you did.'

'Me? But I loved him! And it was Winston he was stealing from.' She trailed off a little as it dawned on her that she was making a revelation, and one not to Ravi's credit.

'I know,' I reassured her. 'But the thing is, Winston told me that before Ravi died. Why would he tell me the reason if he was about to kill him?'

'Arrogance? And even if you do have a point, why would I want to kill him at all?'

'Well… Look, I'm not trying to impugn your relationship. You seemed solid, in the brief time I was around you both. But he also seemed like someone who liked to party, so I'm wondering –'

'About infidelity?' She snorted. 'You're way off. Ravi was very loyal. Very.'

'Everyone thinks that.'

'Not everyone has proof.'

'What do you mean?'

'He had no reason to stray, because his leash wasn't that short.'

'Oh?'

'Yeah.'

'So he could… and you could?'

'Yeah. Monogamy isn't natural, we didn't want to limit each other that way. Not sexually, anyway.'

I sat for a while, digesting this. It was incredibly galling. Not only did the two of them have perfect hair and perfect bodies, but they'd been in love since school *and* they got to play the field. Meanwhile, the rest of us were stuck just trying to find one single viable partner. But I guess I didn't need to be jealous of them any more.

'But are you sure he always, you know, kept to the rules of your arrangement?'

'He was pretty honourable about it. He always came to me after and told me the details. Maybe too many details. Like, with recorded visual aids. Ever since school.'

'Gosh.'

'Yeah, so, not a lot of reason to think I might have killed him for cheating on me.'

'No. No, I can see that.' Although, actually, I *could* imagine wanting to kill someone after years of them showing me videos of their other encounters, whatever permission I had given them beforehand. Bella was talking a good game, but, at the same time, if she had killed him, she would have had to figure out her line on this beforehand. And organise a scapegoat. Not to mention witnesses… But then, why kill Mrs Flyte? Or the Strangs?

We sat in silence, while I twiddled the fraying corner of a towel and she stared at her red hands.

'I guess you probably want to shower.'

She roused herself, but then slumped back again.

'It's strange. I mean, it's horrible having this blood on me, I can smell it and seeing it makes me think of him, all mangled. But also…When I kneeled down in this blood it was still warm. And it's like, if I wash it off, that's the end somehow. For Ravi. That's the end.'

By now she was crying, and I was standing next to her, making small comforting noises, one hand on her shoulder. I waited until she had sobbed herself out. Then she nodded at me and stood up to go and shower. I turned and walked past the tartan-covered bed and the tartan-curtained window and left the room.

CHAPTER 16

I closed the door gently behind me and leaned against it, waiting till I heard a faint swoosh of water before setting off down the hall. Outside Mrs Flyte's room, I paused, imagining what I would see if I went in. James had covered her as we were leaving, what now seemed like a lifetime ago. Perhaps because of that, I couldn't picture her bare, dead face any more, but the spectral shape of her eye sockets pouching the sheet was more frightening than any rictus would have been. I breathed shallowly, hoping not to catch the whiff of decay. Fortunately, it was cold in the house, and getting colder. It would be a bitter night.

But it wasn't Mrs Flyte's room I wanted to visit. I strode along, past mange-eaten stag's heads, burned-out bulbs and faux-ancestral portraits in cracked frames, until I reached the door labelled 'The Heather Room'. Penny's. I double-checked the brass tag on the key I was holding, put it in and turned the handle. I stepped through and, oh, so quietly – I didn't want to be caught – closed it behind me. And then I turned to face my dead friend's things.

Like James's room, this one was suited to its occupant. Or former occupant. Everything was a shade of mauve, lilac or orchid. Nick and I had always ridiculed Penny for her old-womanish taste, every droopy pullover and shapeless skirt a shade that was somehow drabber than grey. I could barely see her clothes at first; they blended so perfectly into the upholstery.

I started by going through her suitcase. It was tidy, much tidier than any bag or drawer of mine had ever been. Each garment was neatly folded and stacked, with socks and books tucked in around the edges to prevent anything from moving in transit. It was almost untouched: just one pile a little out of alignment, as though she'd dug around at the bottom for some wanted item.

What I was looking for wasn't in the suitcase, so I turned to the rest of the room. This, too, was freakishly tidy, at least by my standards. No wet towels on the floor, no dirty socks balled up and tossed into opposite corners. One ashes-of-roses pullover neatly draped across the back of a chair. A book on the bedside table: *The Woman in White* – she'd always liked fat novels. A glass of water.

No note. That's what I was here for – to see if Penny had left an explanation. To see if that explanation mentioned me.

I opened the wardrobe and ran my fingers along the upper shelves. I checked the bathroom and rummaged in her make-up case, making bottles and brushes clack against each other. Nothing.

In the waste-paper basket, though, I struck lucky. Or unlucky, maybe, depending on how you looked at it. Among crumpled tissues and a discarded train ticket was a balled-up piece of lined paper with a torn edge that indicated it had come out of a diary. I smoothed it on the desk and read it with the sound of the wind and the rain in my ears.

Not that there was much to read. It wasn't a note so much as the draft of a note, half of the words scribbled out, lines skipped between false starts.

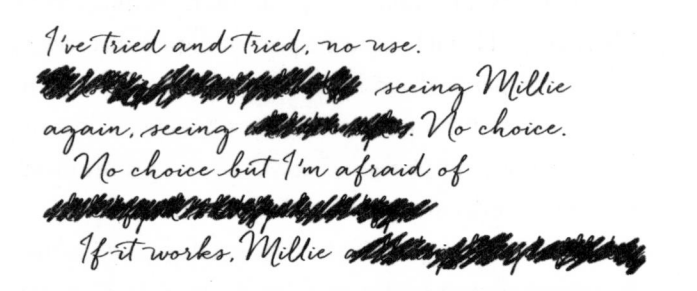

I wasn't happy to see my name in Penny's writing, but it wasn't too damning. There was nothing there that indicated what had happened last year before we both left Flights. I thought of her tear-stained face leaning over her cocktail glass that last night when we'd really spoken to each other, and I winced. I should have been a better friend.

But the police didn't know how guilty I felt, and this rough draft of a note didn't tell them much. It was probably safe to crumple it back up and leave it in the bin for them to find. They'd assume I was mentioned because we'd known each other before. I could tell them we'd talked about how depressed she was, only I hadn't realised she was that fragile. It would be an adequate explanation.

Only, of course, I realised as I balled the sheet up again, it wouldn't explain my fingerprints on the paper. And would that look bad? My heart started racing; my breath shortened. I looked around the room, thinking of everything I'd touched. I pulled my sleeve down over my hand and rubbed at every flat surface I had felt in my search. The clothes and make-up might be all right – I could always say I'd borrowed something the night before.

But there was no rubbing my prints off this almost-note, and therefore, if I left it behind, no pretending I hadn't seen it. My mouth was parched and I couldn't think straight, couldn't decide on the best thing to do. In the end I obeyed instinct and shoved the crumpled note deep into the pocket of my jeans. I could find somewhere to destroy it later.

Leaving, I turned the key in the lock and then paused while my heartbeat slowed back down, my brain stuttering over the locking action for some reason that wasn't clear to me at first. Then it crystallised: I hadn't needed the gesture going in, because the lock hadn't needed undoing. The door had been open. I suppose Penny might not have locked it behind her, going out for the last time. Then I thought of the pile of clothes slightly misaligned, the one make-up brush I'd noticed lying out, next to the tidied, zipped-up case. Signs of use I had put down to Penny's own hand, but might they instead be traces of someone else's presence? Someone who got there before me.

I remembered Winston's remark about Bella, and how she should have been able to see the door to their room from where she claimed to have been sitting. She should have been. But she wouldn't have, if, while Ravi was being killed, she was in this room, going through Penny's things, effecting the same search that I had just carried out.

I thought of my own quick-beating heart and spinning brain, the panic I'd just felt at the idea of being caught. Bella might have felt those things, too, and then left that room, relieved, too eager to get out of there to remember to lock the door. Only to find Ravi dead and bloodied on her return.

At least she didn't find the note. Only, it occurred to me as I went back down the hall to replace Penny's key in the office: maybe she did. Or maybe she didn't find the draft. Maybe she found the final version. And what might that have said?

Bella wasn't the only one who needed a shower. My fisherman's pullover, acquired for the trip and worn for all my fantasy clifftop walks, was bloody and ruined. I stood in the hall, flushed from illicit activity, and pulled it off. But even without it, I *felt* filthy. Washing would probably only help so much, but it was worth a try, so I headed back to my room, thoughts tripping from death to death, from the pills to the axe to the note, from my suspicions about Bella to those I harboured about Winston and even, more reluctantly, about James.

It would have been so much easier if there was just one person to fear. But they had all been dishonest, all given me reason to be wary. I huddled under the trickle of the electric shower, hoping to find some clarity in its ungenerous heat.

Everyone had provoked my suspicions – but not to the same degree. Winston was at the top of my list of suspects. As I examined my reasons, I had to admit that the inquisitorial guise that he adopted towards me was probably a big part of it. I didn't like the shadows he cast on my motives, so I cast shadows on his. The only clear dishonesty I had detected was his implication that he'd been drinking alone last night, when I'd found two glasses in the library. All the same, he had an obvious motive for killing Ravi, and he had been present for what he claimed was Penny's suicide. He was strongly implicated in two of the deaths that had occurred, and I was struggling to believe that it was coincidence. Especially as I reflected on his manner on the clifftop, when he'd taken us to see Penny's body – cold and sardonic. Almost as though what he was really interested in was the amusement to be had from watching our reactions. And if he had decided to create that amusement for himself again?

On the other hand, he wasn't the only one to have found a body. In fact, now that I reflected, I realised that all three of the people left in the house with me had done. James had found Mrs Flyte, another death that was looking more like murder since Ravi had been killed. I couldn't help wondering about his involvement there. After all, who better than a pharmacist to mess around with someone's drugs? And drugs were his whole reason for being here, which made him doubly suspicious to a law-abiding citizen like me. But then, he'd been so willing to point out the switched pills, which he surely wouldn't have done if the switch was his own doing. I wanted to believe he was innocent, but I couldn't deny that, just as Winston's prickliness towards me brought out a certain prickliness towards him, I felt a softness towards James that might be clouding my judgement. He'd been so friendly, so helpful, so understanding, ever since we arrived. It couldn't just be manipulation, could it?

Then there was Bella. I'd taken against her from the start; I couldn't deny that. She was pretty, successful, and arrogant to boot. In my own lonely, messed-up state, her shiny life felt like an insult. I couldn't imagine that someone with everything in front of them like that would throw it all away in a jealous rage, and she'd explained away that possibility pretty frankly. But, contained in that revelation of her and Ravi's – I wasn't sure what to call it exactly: liberated? freaky? – lifestyle, there was another. He did sleep with other women. Maybe she'd just had enough? At the very least, she'd lied about where she was while he was dying. Why?

But, as with James, I didn't want to believe she'd done it. Bella still irritated me, but I'd begun to see something different in her. Her affection for Ravi had seemed like the one genuine thing in an internet-airbrushed life, and her grief when she'd sobbed against my chest after finding him had seemed just as real.

And what about me? I didn't think the others had any reason to be suspicious of me, but as Winston had made clear when he questioned us in the kitchen, we had all been out of each other's sight for long enough to kill. And, in my own way, I was being dishonest. I had no plans to tell them about Penny's note, or about the reasons for which I was looking for it in the first place.

I switched off the inadequate shower, wringing out my hair and shivering in the instant embrace of cold air. In spite of my chill, the mirror had steamed up, and I raised a hand to swipe the clouds away and reveal my own face, expecting a disappointing vision, wan with fear and fatigue. But I stopped before I could bring it to light. Almost invisible in the light of the dull bulb, showing only as fainter steam against steam, a word had been scrawled into my mirror, a word that hadn't been there last time I used the shower.

The word was 'Guilty'.

CHAPTER 17

Guilty. My fingers paused before the mirror and gave a little jerk, as though about to trace the word. But it was already fading, as cold air cut through the dispersing steam. Soon I was left with a clear mirror bearing no accusatory script, just the dismayed image of my own frightened face.

There was an obvious explanation, but I didn't want to confront it, so I concentrated on other possibilities. *Did I write that myself?* In the tense atmosphere of the house, in a moment of absence, could my psyche have found some relief in tracing that word on the mirror? I hoped so, because the possibility that somebody had sneaked in here while I was ignorantly (though not blissfully) ensconced behind the shower curtain, distracted by my own thoughts and the meagre supply of hot water, and written in the steam in order to scare me, to accuse me – it was too chilling to contemplate.

Except, of course, that my mind couldn't leave the possibility alone. The probability, even. But who knew what *I* had to feel guilty about? Penny, who was now dead. Unless… Had someone seen me coming out of her room and pieced something together? The corridor had been empty, and I'd been wary of being seen. Still, perhaps somebody peeping out from around an almost-closed door could have spotted something. Bella had only been down the hall; she might have had time to sneak out, hide herself in a nearby room and watch. She'd seemed pretty preoccupied with her own affairs, though: chiefly, the matter of washing off Ravi's blood. And if anyone had acted suspicious of me on this trip, it was Winston, not her.

But not everyone needs an open door to see. Suddenly I was seized by the irrational fear that those restless spirits I had scoffed at over lunch were real. Real and watching. The December cold no longer seemed an adequate explanation for the icy air of the bathroom. The shower curtain rippled a little. It must be a draught. It must be, but I couldn't bring myself to push it back and look. I shut my eyes tight and clutched my towel tighter, whispering to myself, '*I* wrote it. I did it. It was me.'

But then, if I had written it myself, why? Did I really have so much to feel guilty for? *Yes, you've got plenty*, replied an unhelpful inner voice. And it was true; there was a long list. I hadn't appreciated my father enough when he was alive. I barely spoke to my mother, who still was. Not to mention all the people from Flights. Talking to Penny and Nick these past days had reminded me of the ignoble end of my time there. Poor Penny, so distraught when she was losing her job, and I had been more concerned with keeping mine than being a friend to her. Fat lot of good it had done me in the end. I had ended up unemployed shortly after her, when the Strangs decided to wind up the charity. And hadn't I resented them for it? Another thing to feel guilty about, now that they were dead. So, yes, plenty. I looked myself hard in the eye, in the mirror that no longer bore any kind of verdict. *Now you know what you think of yourself, my dear.*

Still, there was nothing to do now but to brush the past off and try to do better. I let the cold tail of my wet hair down from its towel and, shivering, considered the clothes I had left to wear. Something in me felt defiant, so I hurried into the dress I'd brought for the party, a short lamé number that hugged my curves and showed off my back. I dried my hair carefully, made up my eyes and checked my tights for runs. I looked pretty good, actually.

The effect was somewhat spoiled when I realised I'd be freezing and shrugged on a loose black pullover over the dress, but I still felt emboldened. I'd expected to need this confidence to face a crowded hall full of exciting people I'd never met. The challenge I was facing had turned out to be somewhat different, but I still wanted to feel I was making the most of myself.

I headed for the kitchen, and, when I got there, I found that Winston and James had obeyed the same instinct and were wearing party clothes like some kind of armour. Winston, unsurprisingly, had a tuxedo that fitted too perfectly to be rented. James's get-up was more casual, but he wore it well: a white shirt and a deep-green jacket that brought out glints of the same shade in his hazel eyes. My own eyes wanted to rest on him, but I looked away and spoke to cover my confusion.

'It's been a while since that toast, huh?'

Supper time was approaching, but there was now nothing to eat. Still, we weren't hungry enough yet to open the ancient fish paste. Especially after seeing a dead body. The police would be here, surely, by tomorrow morning at the latest. They would take us away to a safer and better victualled location. Still, it didn't help with the general nervousness, being so low on supplies.

'I could have sworn there was more in the freezer earlier,' said James. 'Didn't you see some sweetcorn, Millie? I thought we could make a casserole with the tuna, American style. But now I can't find the tuna, either.'

'Someone's given it to the cat.' Winston pointed to the floor by the sink, where a tin with a peeled-back lid had obviously been licked clean.

'Ah.' James kept opening cupboards, confirming their emptiness and banging them shut, until Winston said sharply:

'Are you experimenting with the musical possibilities of cupboard percussion?'

'Sorry. I just keep hoping there'll be something in there. Or that something will be different, that it'll all have been just a dream, you know?'

I nodded, embroidering on my own, similar wishes.

'We'll walk into the other room, and the party will be going ahead just as planned. Okay, maybe with slightly worse decor and canapés than I was picturing before I came here, but…'

'A normal disappointment,' said James. 'Maybe even something – or someone – better than you expected.'

I looked at him sharply, wondering if this last comment meant something for my particular benefit. But then I followed his gaze to the door, and my heart sank. It couldn't be me who was the 'someone better' than he had expected. Not when Bella looked like *that*.

She was in gold, like me, but that was where the resemblance ended. Her hair cascaded down in perfect waves, blending with the dress. It was a full coverage affair, reaching to the floor and down her arms in sheer, floaty, feathery layers of fabric that suggested just as much as they concealed. It was a magical dress, and obviously very expensive. I had been pleased with my cheap-and-cheerful look, but next to Bella, all I looked was cheap. My dress was too tight, too shiny, too obvious – something a student would wear to a nightclub. Hers was worthy of an awards ceremony. I tugged my hemline down and tried not to see what effect she was having on James.

'Nothing to eat?' she asked. We shook our heads. 'Doesn't matter. I feel like I need to cleanse, anyway.'

She crossed to Mrs Flyte's favourite cupboard, chandelier earrings tinkling in the otherwise silent kitchen. She opened it and extracted a bottle of whisky from among the collection.

'Anyone else feel like burning out the toxicity?'

'I *could* have put it better myself,' said Winston, 'but I couldn't agree more with the sentiment.'

'Isn't it a bit odd, though?' I looked around them, knowing one of them was a murderer, hoping this time I'd see it spelled out on somebody's face. They stared back at me blankly. 'I mean, knowing what we know about each other. Knowing what's upstairs. It seems strange to have a drink together.'

James shuffled his feet and cleared his throat, looking uncertainly to the others before he spoke.

'You're right. But the way I see it is – there's no way I'm going off on my own in this house after what's happened.'

'Once again,' said Winston, 'I am surprised to find myself in complete agreement with one of you.'

'What they said.' Bella waggled the bottle first at one man, then the other. I nodded.

'Well okay then. Let's have a drink.'

We gathered glasses and Bella sloshed a generous measure into each. She raised hers, swirling the caramel-coloured liquid around in it, holding it up to the light.

'To those who are now spirit.'

Winston rolled his eyes but held his glass up too, and said:

'To fallen comrades.'

'To those who have gone on before us,' said James. I wanted to think of something poetic or witty to cap the toast, but, in the end, I couldn't improve on a classic.

'To absent friends.' Our glasses chinked, we drank, and I hoped to God that the burn of whisky going down would wipe out some of what had happened in the past two days. Or the past year, for that matter.

We proceeded to get drunk. Whisky followed whisky, and soon there were a couple of empty bottles on the mantelpiece in the library, where we had repaired at a point I could no longer quite remember.

As I poured the last drop from another bottle into my glass, Bella shouted at me to go back into the kitchen for more.

'Get another one! This is no time to be sober.'

'She's right, you know.' Winston was slurring, too, but it hadn't made him any less condescending. 'You should listen to sense when you hear it.' He nodded at his own wisdom and knocked back what was left in his glass.

''Strue,' affirmed James. ''Snewyear's, affer all.'

'Okay, okay, I'm going.' Somehow leaving the circle of the fire to brave the darkness of the house didn't appeal to me. But in my whisky-fuddled state, I couldn't quite remember why. 'Aren't we meant to stick together, though?'

'I'll come with,' said Bella, struggling to her feet amid the many layers of her dress. She wasn't the person whose company I'd been hoping for, but it was better than going out there alone.

In the kitchen, I stared into the whisky cupboard, now considerably less full than it had been when I first saw Mrs Flyte open it.

'Do you think one more bottle's enough?' I asked Bella over my shoulder.

'Oh Jesus.' When I turned, a little unsteadily, she was bent over and sobbing intensely. It was over before I could make my way across the room. Righting herself, she stared at the makeshift mirror formed by the night-darkened window and made a vain attempt to wipe the runnels of eye make-up off her cheeks. She smiled at her transparent reflection: a painful smile, all teeth. "Sokay. I'm just thinking of Ravi. He woulda made this… He knew how to have a good time.'

I hiccupped and nodded.

'Let's go knock one back for him.'

The whole house was freezing now. Whatever Mrs Flyte had done to keep it feebly heated wasn't being done any more. Despite my whisky jacket, I shivered as we crossed the hall, thinking what it must be like outside.

Back in the library, though, with a fire burning away and gently lighting our empties from below, it was warm. The cat was in the room, twining around our ankles as we clinked glasses once again. I reached for it and tried to give it a good rub between the ears, but it snarled and batted me away with its claws out, before running off.

The sight of blood beading slowly on my hand made me feel suddenly sick and unpleasantly sober. I dropped onto the sofa, clutching my stomach and my head queasily. James looked over, asking in a concerned slur if I was all right. I nodded dismissively, because I didn't want to tell him the truth.

It wasn't the drink, or the stuffy room. It was that I'd remembered one of us was a murderer. For a couple of hours, the whisky had eclipsed my knowledge of the bodies upstairs, one peaceful, one mangled. Even when Bella mentioned Ravi, I'd thought of him abstractly, as someone absent, not lying mutilated on the tiles upstairs. But with the sight of blood – how had I forgotten? Why was I laughing with them, celebrating like it was just another New Year's party? Was that really the kind of person I was? Could I ignore evil in my pursuit of a good time?

Was that why my mirror had called me guilty?

The others were still talking. Their uneasy laughter seemed sinister. The whisky pounded in my head, the room spun in a queasy montage of images from the past days: a body in the water, a body on the bed, a body covered in blood, the bloody scratch on my hand… I was about to cry out, to tell them to *Stop, stop, I want to get off*, when –

Crashhhhh.

This time I recognised the sound of the gong. But I was more terrified than the last time it had surprised me. Because no one could have struck it. Everyone alive in the house was here in this room.

CHAPTER 18

Now I wasn't the only one sobering up. The others looked fearfully at one another. I could see the same remembered images that had been making my head spin coming back to them, too, the same questions – *How could I have forgotten, how could I have been chatting so calmly with these people?* – being asked in each bleary, frightened mind.

'Did you do that?' Winston asked me.

'Why is it always me you accuse? And no, obviously.'

'We've gotta go look,' said James. None of us made a move.

'Okay,' I said. 'On three. We all go to the hall together. One, two, three.'

I was the only one who went towards the door. My annoyance, combined with the whisky still coursing through my system, was for a moment stronger than my fear. But it quickly began to ebb, and the thing that eventually made me step into the hall was a foolish desire not to lose face.

Nothing immediately happened to me, and I could feel the other three crowding behind my back.

We stood very still, quite small in the large space. Cold draughts sent clots of dust spinning across the tiled floor. The gong shimmered slowly to a stop, but nothing stirred in the shadows. There wasn't anything to see, but that absence was frightening. I felt my nape prickling. The others *were* gathered right behind me, but was that the only reason? Was somebody else – something else – poised there, waiting in the dark? I strained to hear beyond my own breath. Slow creaks, rustles. *Please just let those be the noises made by an old house.*

My heartbeat hadn't slowed since the gong sounded, and it leaped into my throat, nearly choking me with fear, when Bella whispered:

'I think we should revisit the ghost theory.'

Then a door slammed on the floor above. Primed by the gong, the whisky and the strain of the past few days, something in me broke out into a scream.

Eventually I stopped. My arms were around my head, and I was half-bent in a crash position. As the high note of my shriek faded, I heard not whatever ghoulish menace I'd been expecting, but laughter. I uncurled and saw James leaning against the doorframe, gasping, and Bella and Winston smirking at me too. My first thought was resentful.

'Is this some sort of practical joke?'

'No,' said James. 'Look, he's done it again.'

He pointed across the hall to the dining-room door, where, peeking around the doorframe and then licking his paw with the characteristic nonchalance of a cat trying to convince you he'd meant to do something, was the ginger tom.

'Well, that's a relief,' said Winston. 'Considering that the alternative was…'

'Was that we weren't alone in the house,' I finished for him.

It was a relief. Nonetheless, the possibility of a spectre had thoroughly frightened me, even if it was laid to rest almost as soon as it was raised. Fear and embarrassment coursed through me, replacing the whisky in my blood. When we returned to the library, the atmosphere – never very convivial, but at least sort of grimly gregarious – had dissolved. We sat, stiff, anxious, casting wary glances at each other.

'What time is it?' asked James.

Winston looked at his watch, a fine gold affair with a black leather strap.

'Ten o'clock.'

'Not long till the new year. Hopefully it'll start better than this one ended.' I smiled at the others as I said it, but no answering smiles rewarded me. Even James, the most accommodating of my remaining companions, remained silent and dour, his gaze turned inward. My grin began to slide. I could feel whisky burning my otherwise empty stomach. My mouth tasted sour and old, and my head was thick. The drunken giddiness had gone completely out of me, but there was still too much booze in my blood to let me think straight. It was sickening, being trapped nearly sober in a drunk body. I had to sleep.

'I've got to go to bed.' I struggled to my feet, stumbling in my heeled shoes.

'Not so fast.' Winston reached out and grabbed my wrist, yanking me to a halt. I tugged to free myself, but his grip was unyielding.

'Let me go! What the hell?'

'I've no wish to restrain you for the sake of it. The mood is all wrong for bondage play, and, besides, you're hardly my type. But I think you'll recall we agreed not to leave each other's sight until the police arrive.'

'Did we?' I sat down and shook off his hand, nursing my wrist with what was probably a childishly sulky expression. 'We've already been out of each other's sight, though. We all showered and changed.'

'An excellent point. But, not to descend to cliché, that was then, and this is now. We all made it out of our ablutions alive. Surely you don't want anyone else succumbing to… let's call it the bad air. Not before morning, when the police must at long last arrive?'

'Of course not. But also… I want some rest.' I looked at the other two, staring listlessly into sticky glasses. 'Aren't you all tired?' James slowly raised his head.

'I don't think I've ever been more exhausted in my life.' He drained his glass.

'The thing is,' said Bella, standing and going over to the fire, carefully setting another empty bottle in the row before spinning back around and facing us. 'I don't care about keeping my eye on these two. It's you I'm not letting out of my sight.' She levelled a finger at Winston, who raised his eyebrows and pressed a hand to his chest in mock protest.

'*Moi?* Well, what a convenient set of matched suspicions. I'm not taking my eyes off you, either.'

'You think *she* did it?' I squawked in surprise. 'But this whole time, you've been acting so suspicious of me.'

'I am. I'm suspicious of all of you. We all could have done it. But let's say I think the simplest solution is usually the right one.'

'But…' My brain was struggling against the whisky. 'If it's just you watching each other, who, you know, watches the watcher? Doesn't the watcher need to be watched?'

Everyone looked fuddled for a moment, parsing my question to see if it made sense.

'She's right,' said James. 'We can't just leave you two alone.'

We all fell silent, our thoughts making slow progress against the boozy current.

'The on-call room!' James smacked his forehead. 'Like in a hospital. Winston, your room faces mine across the hall. If you keep the door open, and we call out to each other every so often, nothing can happen without being noticed. But everyone can get a bit of rest.'

'My room's too far down the hall,' I objected. 'No one will hear me calling out.'

'You can come in with me, Millie,' said James. 'You have the bed and I'll take the chair. I don't mind.'

I wasn't sure how to react to this. On the one hand, it was very… intimate. There was something brewing between James and me, I thought, or hoped – maybe it was just the drink warming us up. But this was quite an acceleration. At the same time, I was pretty sure that James wasn't the murderer, and I would feel a lot safer if I wasn't alone.

'So where am I sleeping?' Bella frowned, and then her eyes got big. 'I won't go back in that room.' I forbore to point out that she had been happy enough to go and get her party clothes from her suitcase. Sleeping in there all night – that was a different matter.

'Nor should any of us,' said Winston. 'Crime scene and all that. But you should be somewhere within earshot.'

'So, what? I just roll blankets out in the hall between your doors? I sleep on the actual *floor*?' When none of us proffered an alternative, she gave a rasping sigh of disgust and closed her eyes in acquiescence. 'This has already been the most awful weekend of my life; may as well get a little bit worse. Let's go.'

We trooped upstairs. While James gallantly made up a little sleeping place in the hall, and Winston leaned against the wall, pointedly not helping, Bella pulled me aside.

'I think you should sleep in the hall with me,' she said, in a drunkenly indiscreet whisper. 'Don't go in a room with him. He could be, you know, *the one*.'

'I don't think he is, though,' I hissed back. 'Other people have better reasons.' I looked meaningfully at Winston, though I could just as easily have been referring to her.

'I guess.' She stared at Winston a moment and then shrugged and plucked her large earrings one by one from her ears. 'I still think you're being stupid. But I'm too tired to teach you better.'

Bella nestled into her blankets on the floor, and, between the facing doors where we'd spend the night, the rest of us paused awkwardly. It seemed like a moment, but no one was sure what to say. Eventually I settled for:

'See you in the morning.'

'If we make it that long,' said Winston, grinning.

We turned. Winston went into his room, and I stepped with James into his.

CHAPTER 19

We left the door open. It felt like a date in the 1950s. Winston did likewise, across the way, and Bella decided to test our system by kicking the wall.

'Did you hear that?'

'Yup,' called James.

'No one's going to get away with murder, then,' shouted Winston. 'At least, not another one.' His voice faded. I could just hear Bella outside the door; she was bitching quietly about how uncomfortable she was.

I sat gingerly on the edge of the tartan coverlet, my hands tucked beneath my thighs. James sighed and sank into the armchair. He switched on the table lamp and rubbed his face in his hands.

'You can have first sleep, if you like. Feel free to use the bathroom, whatever you need.'

'Thanks. You don't have... no, it's weird, never mind.'

'What?'

'Well, I didn't think to get anything from my room, to sleep in. But it sort of seems like we're in for the night, if you know what I mean.'

'Of course, and you in your party clothes – not ideal pyjamas. Have a T-shirt.' He crossed to the dresser and extracted one.

In the bathroom, I rubbed toothpaste around my mouth with a finger, amused at how the sensation brought back my student days. However much of a mess my life had become, it was a long time since I'd failed to brush my teeth properly. I did my best to clean my make-up off with only cold water and a hand towel. I pulled the T-shirt on. James was well built, and it hung as low as a nightgown on me. The fabric smelled of sandalwood, laundry soap, maleness. A good smell, the kind of smell I hadn't had a chance to enjoy for a year.

Back in the room, his eyes were closed, and his head was thrown back against the chair, light tracing the line of his profile. I slipped under the covers quietly, unsure whether he had fallen asleep. I had been exhausted when we came up the stairs, but now I found my mind buzzing, my body alive to the sensation of his shirt against my skin, his pillow pressed softly against my cheek.

'Do you want the light off?' he asked.

'Oh, uh, sure. I guess it would help.'

A click, and the room fell dark. Well, darker – the hall lights were still on, but only a faint light reached us, enough to pick out shapes but not colours.

I saw James cross the room. Once again, his profile was outlined in light as he approached the open doorway. Leaning out, he called gently,

'Still alive?'

'So far,' came Bella's answer.

He sat back down. I shut my eyes and tried to settle. I could feel my physical weariness; being cold and hungry and frightened for hours had taken a toll. But my mind wouldn't quiet. Memories and questions kept surging up; the surface stayed choppy. I sighed and turned in the bed.

'Can't sleep?' He said it softly, as though reluctant to wake me in case he was wrong.

'It's funny. I was so exhausted. I still am, really. But my head seems too full to sleep.'

'Full of what?'

'You can guess.'

A groan was his only reply. I shifted in the bed again, hoping that he would say something. In the end, I decided to speak myself.

'James?'

'Yes?'

'This thing that's happened… Do you think – I mean do you have a sense –'

'Do I have a guess as to who did it?'

'Yeah.'

'God, Millie, I don't know.' He was quiet for a while, except for the sounds of his shifting in the chair, which communicated enough of his discomfort. 'I mean, I don't think you did it.'

'Thanks, I guess.'

'I notice you're not returning the compliment.'

'Oh, sorry!' I laughed a little, surprised at the lightness of this of all conversations. I carried on in an undertone, anxious not to be heard across the hall. And anxious to be believed, because I wasn't quite as sure of his innocence as I'd like to be. 'I don't think you did. I mean, the other two have… reasons.'

'Motive, of course. It's all meant to come back to that, isn't it?'

'You know, Winston told me that Ravi had been playing fast and loose with his finances. He volunteered the information, before Ravi was even dead. Why would he do that, if he was going to kill him for it?'

'Double bluff?'

'I suppose. But he didn't seem angry, like someone who wanted vengeance. More…'

'Contemptuously amused?'

'Exactly! That's him, isn't it?'

'The man himself.' Again, he fell silent. I stared into the semi-darkness, my eyes now able to pick out more detail in the room: the fall of the curtains, the glint of the mirror and, near the door, where it was brightest, the night-time ghosts of garish tartan. James cleared his throat and asked,

'Bella, then?'

'I mean, no one could have been closer to Ravi. And it always makes sense to look to the partner in a murder.'

'Does it now?'

'You're right. What do I know?'

'Quite a lot about birds.'

I was glad of the dark, so he couldn't see me blush.

'They're kind of my thing.'

'But not just birds. You're also pretty observant when it comes to people.'

The blush deepened.

'So, you're inclined to believe me when I say I don't think Bella did it, in spite of her being an obvious suspect?'

'I am.'

'Because of the skills I've honed through birdwatching.'

'That, and the fact I'm not sure she did it, either. It's a puzzle, though. One of them must have done it.'

'Or one of us.'

'You're not confessing to me now, are you?'

'No, but… Can I ask you something? It's a little blunt.'

'We've seen corpses and got drunk together. You can speak frankly.'

Even so, I found myself hesitant to voice my question. I didn't want to shatter the atmosphere building in the room. It was something to do with being in the dark, speaking of the others, using low voices. Intimate. What I was about to say might destroy that.

'I don't think it was you or anything… But I did just wonder about Mrs Flyte's pills.'

I had come at it as obliquely as I could, but he understood me anyway.

'Whether I replaced them? Because of my… profession?'

I was listening for resentment or offence in his voice, but his tone was the same as before: tired and neutral in spite of the darkness of what we were discussing and the room we were in.

'Yes, that. And I thought there was a bit of an implication…'

I broke off, afraid to name the reason he'd come here.

'That I don't always practise with, let's say, medical ethics in mind?' Now there was tension in his voice, and I kept quiet, unsure how to respond. That was what I had been asking about, but now that it was out in the open, I didn't know what to say. He sighed.

'It's true. I've been known to use my professional position to… facilitate access to certain substances.'

'To deal drugs.'

'You warned me you'd be blunt; I suppose I can't complain. I came here with my own supply, though. I didn't need to take the pills out of an old lady's bottle. Also, beta blockers… Not a great high.'

I sat up and switched on the bedside lamp. I wanted to see his face, to look for any sign of duplicity. I didn't want to be misled by my desire to find him innocent. He stared back at me, gaze open, a little challenging, but not shifty or reluctant.

'I believe you.'

'That's a relief.'

'Sorry to ask, but surely you understand –'

'It wasn't sarcasm, Millie. I'm genuinely relieved you don't think I did it.'

The blush was back. We remained there, looking at each other, while I felt it spread over my hastily washed, whisky-bleared face. There was no way I looked good in that moment, but the way he was looking at me – it almost seemed as if he thought I did.

'Dark deeds afoot?' Winston was calling from across the hall, no doubt prompted by seeing the light come on.

'Not unless you think getting a glass of water is a dark deed,' I called out, smiling at James. But I immediately felt compunction; I'd been asking for his honesty, and here I was fibbing, however innocently. I got up and crossed to the sink, suddenly very aware of my bare legs. I filled the tooth-glass and drank, feeling a little more of the whisky ebb out of my blood. Then I hurried back under the covers, shivering in the cold room. I kept the light on, however, and stayed sitting up, looking at James, who hadn't moved in the chair.

Then something occurred to me. I listened for a moment, wondering whether the others were eavesdropping, but all I heard was a tiny snore from Bella on the floor outside. I spoke, quieter than before.

'So, if you came here to… supply, then you weren't invited by friends?'

James looked to the corridor, too, then got up and came over to the bed, sitting on top of the duvet in front of me.

'It was a job. I have a kind of portal; people can get in touch. Someone wrote and described the situation, said I could come and attend the party, just act like one of the guests. All expenses paid, as long as I brought some things to help the atmosphere along.'

'But weren't you suspicious? That it was a police trap or something?'

'You get a feel for these things. I mean, it makes sense, right? How many drug dealers are there on remote, uninhabited Scottish islands? It's not like they could deliver, and punters often feel uncomfortable carrying around loads of bags of white powder. I probed a bit, but I do gigs like this all the time.' He paused and looked down, tracing the different lines of the duvet's tartan pattern. 'Obviously, I should have asked more questions. But in one way it has been worth it.'

And then he looked up at me, really *at* me, and I couldn't mistake his meaning.

I caught my breath. I leaned in, transfixed. His eyes, his mouth.

Only…

CHAPTER 20

'Wait,' I said.

James leaned back, blinking a little. Now it was his turn to blush. Part of me was cursing myself. I couldn't believe I'd cut off the kiss. My first in a year, and there was no guarantee there'd be another one. But I had to understand.

'Sorry. It's just... I get that you didn't do anything to Mrs Flyte, and you came here with, maybe not the most innocent of intentions, but at least not murderous ones. But I just don't understand. How can you do the job you do, so responsible and everything, and then sell drugs on the side?'

He gave a crooked half-smile, so at least I hadn't completely put him off.

'I know, I don't seem the type. But life has a way of putting you in awkward positions.'

I shifted under the blanket, waiting for him to continue.

'It's this.' He stretched out his prosthetic leg and tapped

the shin lightly against the bedside table, just enough to make a small metallic sound. 'Life was different before this.'

'You seem to get around pretty well.'

'Sure, I've learned how to work with it. And I was always a bit of a daredevil. That's what lost me the leg.' Again, he paused, staring at the limb.

'You don't have to tell me.'

'It's all right. It's just strange to talk about it. Most people want to pretend it isn't there. So did I for a long time.' He sighed and laid back across the bed, closing his eyes. 'It changed who I was going to be.

'I wanted to be a doctor, not a pharmacist. Nothing wrong with my profession; it's very useful. But doctors have the glamour. I thought I'd be one of those ones you see in war zones or developing countries. You know, striding around in my safari gear and stethoscope, saving people, taking pictures surrounded by smiling locals. A life of romance, adventure and medical sainthood. A big life.'

'It sounds pretty exciting.'

'I thought so. It also sounds like a bit of a cliché, but I suppose most seventeen-year-olds' dreams are clichés.'

'I was expecting to discover a new species, or maybe be a telly naturalist. You know, "Look closely, folks, and you might just see the elusive bittern peering out from between the reeds. What's certain is that you'll hear his distinctive booming call travel across the Broads if you visit during the spring breeding season."'

James smiled.

'It seems so innocent and absurd when you look back at it like that.'

'So, what happened?'

'I couldn't quite wait to get my thrills.' His jaw clenched, as though he were chewing the words before speaking them. 'I had a motorbike. I liked riding it fast. And one day…'

'The accident?'

'The accident.'

I waited, but he didn't seem prepared to go on.

'I'm sorry. But I don't quite see how that led here.'

'Right, the drugs. Well, what you have to understand is that with an amputation, it's not just the pain of the accident, of the operation, of healing. The pain goes on and on, if you're unlucky.'

'Are you talking about a phantom limb?'

'Even more than that: a phantom life. The life that would have been mine if it hadn't happened.'

'But surely you could still be a doctor with one leg?'

'Of course. But with one leg, and a set of bombed exam results, and a couple of years spent out of education, drinking and taking pills and raging at the world? It becomes a little less likely.'

'So, you made it back to school, but without the kind of marks to go into medicine?'

'I did what seemed like the next best thing. And I do like my work. Much more humane hours than all that rushing around conflict zones or working nights in A&E. But still, there's a… a kind of gap.' He shaped the empty air with his hands.

'And you thought extra money might fill it?'

'Money helps. But, more than that, the thrill – taking things, breaking rules, not getting caught. And also…'

'Yes?'

'Have you ever suffered – really suffered?'

I thought of my father dying and the lonely life I'd led since then. I thought of working at Flights, and being friends with Penny, and longing for Nick to notice me, and then no longer being friends with Penny, and watching the charity disappear. I thought of Drew Strang, his magnificent head bloodied and empty after the car accident, and Penny's body beaten by the waves at the foot of the cliff. I thought of the grey mess of my flat, of my life. I nodded.

'Then you know that sometimes the usual things aren't enough. Putting on a cheerful face, telling yourself it'll be all right. Sometimes you need something more. I did. Others do, too. And I didn't feel I could judge them or refuse them. Not after what happened to me.'

I pulled the duvet closer, considering what he'd said. I could see where he was coming from, certainly. And it wasn't as if I hadn't used booze and food to self-medicate over the past year. If you had access to stronger stuff, it probably didn't seem like such a big difference. But it pained me. Reconciling the image I'd had of him – so sociable, skilled and generous – with this darker portrait. He opened one hazel eye and looked at me.

'You're wondering whether you can forgive me?'

I said nothing.

'I don't blame you. Lately I've been feeling like I might not even be able to forgive myself. It's funny, but when I showered and changed – I must have imagined it, but I could have sworn when I got out of the shower someone had written

"Guilty" in the steam of the mirror. Probably just my conscience playing tricks.'

I was glad to hear he had one, but the warm glow of reassurance about his decency was lost in a wash of cold fear. *Guilty.*

'It wasn't.'

'What?'

'It wasn't your conscience playing tricks. I got the same message in the bathroom mirror.'

'What?' This time he sat up and looked at me, wide-eyed. 'So maybe – maybe it *is* ghosts?'

I wanted to smile, but my face felt oddly frozen. We were both silent, listening. I could hear my heartbeat, my blood thumping louder and louder, but there was something else, too. There was a creaking sound coming from somewhere. *Just the house settling on a blustery night. Just that.* My blood thumped louder still.

Then Winston or Bella coughed, and the atmosphere James had called up with the word 'ghosts' eased a little. We looked at each other, rueful.

'Maybe. Or…' I paused, considering whether to give away another potentially incriminating piece of information. 'Winston said he saw something written in Ravi's blood on that mirror, too. He could have…'

'Winston does seem to like messing with people's heads. But then Bella could have, too. Why write on *your* mirror, though? What do you have to be guilty about?'

'Who wrote the message seems like a more important question.'

'That's not fair. I showed you mine.'

There were buttons on the duvet, decorative ones marching down one of the lines of tartan. I twisted one, pulled at it. It was hard to speak. Eventually, James gave me an out.

'You don't *have* to tell me, if it makes you so uncomfortable.'

'No, you're right. You were honest with me. I just… I don't like to think about it. And it feels fresh.' I tore my eyes away from the button, and looked at him. 'It's to do with Penny.'

A change came over his face: distrust. I wondered whether something similar had happened to mine while he was telling his story.

'I don't mean I pushed her or anything! It's not that fresh. But you know we knew each other, before all this happened.'

'You said you worked together.'

'We did. I really loved that job. It was at a charity called Flights of Fancy. A ridiculous name, but we did good work – conservation. We tried to get legislation passed to protect birds and their habitats.'

'Right up your street, then.'

'Exactly. Penny wasn't in it for the birds. She was on the admin side. But it was a good place to work. Our boss was this passionate man; he carried you along with him, made it all feel important. And everyone got along really well. For a while, anyway.'

'What changed?'

'Some people started to get along a little too well.'

'You and…'

I considered telling him a few things, including about Nick. But what was there to tell, really? Nothing, now. Bringing it up would only cloud what was growing between us, which felt like something. 'Penny and our boss.'

'Ah. You did sort of imply something that first night. He was the one who died? In the crash?'

'Him and his wife, yes.'

'So, he and Penny had an affair?'

'And I knew about it. She and I were friends.'

'Really? You seemed pretty awkward together when we first arrived.'

'Things went a bit wrong between us. It was mostly my fault.'

'Even so, I find it hard to imagine. She was such a wallflower, and you're… not that.'

'Flattering as that might be, I haven't always been the social butterfly you see before you.' I was pleased by what he'd said, but then I knew that I'd always shown up well against Penny's dowdiness. If I was honest, it was part of why we'd been friends. 'Maybe you're right, and we wouldn't have been friends if we'd met at school or something. But we were about the same age, worked together, the only two young women in the company. Drew's wife was also there sometimes, but she seemed to find us both pretty uninspiring. So, we were thrown together a lot.'

'Did you guess what was happening?'

'I should have, probably, but no. It blindsided me. I wouldn't have guessed Penny'd have the confidence to have an affair. She'd told me how she was bullied at school, and it kind of seemed like she'd never got over it. As far as I knew, the only person she really loved was her cat. She hid it well, while they were happy.'

'And when they weren't happy any more?'

'I noticed something was off. She kept coming in late, her eyes were red all the time, she would go into Drew's office for long conversations with the door closed. I thought something else had happened, a family tragedy or something, and she was trying to negotiate some time off. You probably think I'm pretty oblivious, huh?'

'Nah, you're sharp as a tack.' His eyes were closed, but he was smiling.

'Not in this case. Anyway, I finally got the picture that something was really wrong, and I told Penny we should go out together and talk. We went for a drink, and she was sort of reluctant. She wouldn't tell me what was wrong. She wouldn't even order anything at first. Finally, I insisted she have a margarita. I was really trying to cheer her up; it seemed more fun than a glass of wine. But when the waitress set it down in front of her, she just burst into tears. So, then it wasn't too hard to get out of her.'

'About the affair?'

'The affair. And the fact that she was pregnant.' James sucked in his breath. 'That made it more complicated. She wanted the baby. He didn't. They were arguing about it every day, but couldn't resolve to do anything. It was a mess.'

'So what did you say?'

'I was too shocked to say much of anything at first. You know how you were surprised that we were friends? That's nothing compared to how surprised I was that they were lovers. He was really... He kind of *glowed*. That's how much presence he had.'

'Opposites attract, I guess.'

'Must be. So, anyway, she's sitting there crying, telling me what's happened, and, I guess absent-mindedly, she's drinking the margarita, even though she shouldn't. And I don't really think about it either, but just keep signalling the waitress to bring more. For both of us. And eventually, we're really, really drunk.'

'Not great, but not necessarily the end of the world in early pregnancy.'

'That was the thing, though. It wasn't actually that early. She'd just been hiding it really well. I think she was maybe five months along? She always liked a baggy jumper.'

'Still, chances are the baby would have been fine.'

'It might have been. But she was in such a state. She was seeing everything in the worst light. You know, thinking everything that could go wrong in her life was going wrong. And, well…'

'What?'

'This is the part I feel guilty about. It's hard to say.'

'Like I said, I showed you mine.'

'Right. Well, we were at a delicate point, at work. We were trying to build momentum to help get some legislation passed; it would have set aside land for rewilding, protected a lot of bird habitats. It wasn't a good time for the wheels to come off. And I may have… highlighted that. You know, "It's such important work we've been doing… You'd hate to ruin that. And if the baby's been harmed by the drinking anyway…"'

'You pressured her to get an abortion?'

'I don't know that I'd exactly put it that way. She was trying to figure out what to do. I just put one case more convincingly than the other.'

'As Winston might have it.'

'Yes.'

'But it was still her decision.'

'I guess. But if I'd been a better friend, I would have cared more about her than about the project. And that's hard to live with, after what's happened. Especially since things kept going wrong for her. I don't know exactly what happened between her and the Strangs, but she left the charity pretty soon after our night out. And then the whole thing fell apart: the legislation didn't pass, there was a weird atmosphere around her leaving, and eventually they decided to wind up the organisation. So, in the end I lost my job, too.'

'Then I'd say you've paid a price. You've nothing to feel guilty about – unless you've seen her since then and done something else you want to tell me?'

'No, I haven't seen her at all. In fact, our New Year's party was the last time I saw her. Exactly a year ago.'

'Speaking of New Year's parties…'

James heaved himself up off the bed, went to the door and called out to the other two. When he got the all-clear, he came back and flopped back down. But he didn't close his eyes this time. He propped himself on an elbow and stared at me.

'What are you thinking?' I asked, twisting my favourite button, afraid to meet his eyes. 'Am I beyond the pale?'

'I'm in no position to judge.'

My eyes flew up.

'Really? I thought you seemed a little… I wondered if you *were* judging me, after Penny died.'

'No! I just felt for you, losing a friend. If I was stand-offish, it was only because I didn't know the right thing to say.'

'So, you won't be writing "Guilty" in the steam on my mirror anytime soon?'

'If I'm in a room you're showering in, there will be other things on my mind.'

I blushed, unsure how to respond. Then Winston shouted from across the hall.

'Oi, you lot! It's midnight.'

And Bella began to sing, still slurring a little.

'*For auld lang syne, my dear, for auld lang syne…*'

James smiled.

'Millie.'

'Yeah?'

'You know what people are supposed to do at midnight on New Year's?'

'I think it's something to do with –'

His broad, warm hand came behind my head and pulled me in. I closed my eyes, and then our mouths met. It was a good kiss, deep and soft, but with a little urgency, a little hunger. I hadn't felt one like it in a year. He pulled back.

'Happy New Year,' he said.

'You know,' I replied, grinning like a fool, 'in spite of everything, after that, I think it just might be.'

NEW YEAR'S DAY

CHAPTER 21

Suddenly I was awake. Things came back to me slowly: where I was, why everything in the room was covered in plaid, how much I must have drunk to leave my mouth tasting the way it did. And then, setting my heart pounding and rudely tearing off the last gentle remnant of sleep, every awful thing that had happened the day before.

Penny, dead. Mrs Flyte, dead. Ravi, really dead.

I felt sick, and it wasn't just the hangover.

But then, as I turned in the bed to get up and find some water, I saw James next to me. And I remembered one more thing. A thing that meant, for the first time in a year or more, becoming conscious wasn't such a disappointment. A thing that gave the day promise, in spite of what had come before.

Now my stomach was struggling with excitement, as well as horror, booze and hunger. But what I really needed to take care of before James woke up was my breath. I slid very carefully out from under the covers and padded across the tartan carpet to the bathroom. I frantically rubbed toothpaste all over my teeth and tongue and rinsed and spat until I had a vague hope that my mouth at least smelled of mentholated roadkill, rather than just roadkill. My face was puffy and pale; there was only so much that splashing with cold water could do. I tried to give myself an encouraging smile in the mirror, tugged James's T-shirt into the most seductive drape I could manage – which wasn't very – and went back out to join him in bed, tiptoeing in the hope that he wouldn't wake up yet.

He was just stirring as I slipped back under the duvet, and I watched the same painful waking process that I had gone through work its changes on him, too. First, he held his head and groaned a bit, then he smiled and reached for me. Mid-gesture, I saw him remember. His arm froze and the humorous light died out in his eyes. He sat up, knees tenting the duvet, and buried his face in his hands. I was relieved when, a moment later, one of those hands made its way across the coverlet towards me.

'Christ, Millie. It just seems like it can't really have happened.'

'But it has.'

'And… What happens next?'

'I guess the police come, we tell them our tale, and –'

'Sure. But I also mean…' He cleared his throat, suddenly reluctant, and played with the fingers of my hand where they were touching his.

'You mean, with me and you?'

'Yes, with us.'

I suppressed a giddy smile at hearing him use the word.

'It's a long ferry ride. I'll need someone to talk to.'

'And after the ferry?'

'It's a long train journey, too.'

We smiled into each other's eyes. Then, once again, he remembered something that clouded over the sunshine in his gaze.

'Hey, we fell asleep. We were supposed to keep watch. Do you think the others did, too?'

'Probably. We were all fairly generous with the whisky last night. It would be pretty heroic to stay awake after that.'

'We should check on them.'

Somehow neither of us wanted to call out. I didn't let myself consider why. Instead, I found an excuse for putting it off.

'We should – but maybe I should go and get some clothes?' I gestured at myself, bare-legged and awash in oversized T-shirt.

'You want to borrow some jeans?'

The jeans were big, though they just about fitted, slung low on my hips and taking two turns of the cuff to clear my feet. But he seemed to find me charming in them.

'Adorable,' he said, helping me into one of his flannel shirts, which hung open over the T-shirt. I held my arm out across the back of the chair: plaid on plaid.

'You might need camouflage,' he said. 'This is a dangerous situation.'

The mood had lightened a little as he dressed me, but this remark, unfortunately true, reminded us of what we had to do.

'Let's see if they're awake.'

Outside, Bella's puddle of blankets and pillows lay abandoned on the floor. Across the hall, Winston's door was open, but no one responded when we called. I hadn't looked at a clock, and it was difficult to tell what time it was by the dim light coming in through the window at the end of the hall. It was no longer fully dark, but this far north in the middle of winter, dawn didn't come particularly early.

After we'd said both their names a few times and received no reply, we nodded to each other and went through the open door. Inside, I began to have a bad feeling – or rather, my days-old bad feeling started getting worse. No one was in the bed, no one was in the bathroom. The room was dark, empty and deserted.

'Where are they?' We had been using our normal voices, but now I found myself whispering.

'We're going to have to go and look.' James was whispering, too, but he tried to smile. 'We're probably panicking over nothing. Bet you anything we'll find them in the kitchen, trying to make breakfast out of potted shrimp or something.'

But we didn't.

We found Bella first. As we rounded the corner of the hall, coming towards the stairs, I saw her outline.

There was nothing surprising about it, really. Not by now. Not after everything else that had happened. Still, instinct is instinct, and I stopped short, my heart beating quickly, no air in my lungs to tell James to stop. He took a moment longer to notice, because he'd been looking at me. He carried on a step and saw I was frozen; then he followed my gaze to the hall mirror. Or what had been the hall mirror.

Now it was a shattered ring of cloudy glass, a fractured mosaic reflecting chaotically around the body in its centre.

Bella had been pushed through it face-first, so that the jagged glass had cut her throat. Blood ran down from the gash, pooling on the carpet. There was just enough space for her forehead to rest on the wall behind, eyes cast down to the pool of blood, throat still sunk on the broken mirror shards. Her body was slumped over the little table that jutted out in front of the mirror, and some distant, calm, pragmatic corner of my brain was surprised that its spindly legs were holding up to the combined weight of the mirror's frame and the woman's corpse.

Her shoes were tumbled on the floor beside her. She must have been on her way to her room, stopped to look at herself, and then…

'Jesus,' breathed James. And, after a moment, 'I guess now we know who did it.'

'So, now the only question is: where is he?'

'I'm right here. And I certainly *did not* do it.' As he spoke, Winston stood up, and I saw that he had been sitting by the banister at the top of the stairs, while we had been taking in the sight of another body. 'Millie, I think you should come over here to me. James, let her go.'

'Are you crazy?' James stepped in front of me protectively. 'I'm not letting you anywhere near her. You're a murderer.'

A little shock went through Winston's body at the final word, as though he'd taken a hit. He drooped and held on to the railing. I stared at him over James's shoulder, fascinated in spite of myself. He had killed Bella; he must have killed Ravi, too, and in the most gruesome way possible. But he didn't look the way a crazed axe-murderer did in my imagination. He seemed deflated, perturbed, less confident than he'd been throughout the whole trip. In a moment, he righted himself and looked straight at me, ignoring James.

'I know it must look bad, but please, my girl, believe me. It's the only way to protect yourself.'

'James couldn't have done this. He was with me all night.'

'And you never fell asleep? You didn't take your eyes off him for one second?'

I felt James stiffen slightly where he stood in front of me. I had done, of course, and a dark flicker of doubt went through my already troubled mind. But no, he had been asleep by my side when I woke up, and his mind had been on other, much nicer things than murder when we had drifted off.

I looked back at Bella's body, and this time I noticed a word smeared through the sticky red drips congealed on what remained of the mirror glass, a word I'd seen on my own mirror before.

'Winston.' I pointed. 'You were the one who told me you saw something written on Ravi's mirror. You wrote it on our mirrors too, didn't you? And then you heard her getting up in the hall, followed her, and did this.'

'But I didn't! My God, I know I've sinned enough in my life, but never anything like this. In matters of transgression, you could say I'm a lover, not a fighter. I can see the point of intoxication, and of sex. But what would I kill for?'

'Ravi... the money...'

'He didn't lose me anything. He just played fast and loose. And even if I were vindictive enough to kill for that, why would I hurt the girl? Or the other girl. Or the old woman. And why would I bring the pair of *you* here? Not to mention the Strangs.'

It was true. I couldn't really think why. But James supplied a reason.

'You killed Bella because she wasn't going to let you get away with it. Nor are we.'

'I wish I could make you believe me. Millie, I'm not the one to be afraid of here. I'm just...' Winston made a strangled noise of frustration and buried his face in his hands. I heard a sharp intake of breath from James, and then he said softly:

'Look, the scratches.'

I saw them: thin welts of dried blood along the backs of Winston's hands. The light was growing in the hall, and there was no trouble picking them out. Traces of where he had pushed Bella through the mirror, killing her.

'Winston,' I said. 'Your hands.'

He raised his head and looked at them, at first bewildered, but then, looking at me, with dismay filling his eyes.

'No, no, it's not what you think. That damn cat. I opened a tin for it, and it tried to claw the food out of my hands before I'd put it down. Then, when I came back up, there she was. I didn't do this to her. I didn't do this!'

Once again, I was struck by the desperation and uncertainty in his tone. This man, usually so well protected behind an armour of unruffled arrogance. But it was impossible to believe him. James had been next to me, and I had been sleeping, so unless I'd murdered her in some somnambulistic episode, there was only one possible conclusion left.

Winston was the murderer.

'Did you push Penny off the cliff?'

There were other questions I could have asked, but this, I realised as I said it, was what really mattered to me. What had they really talked about, sipping whisky late at night in the library? Had Penny really been in such despair that she wanted to kill herself? Did I really deserve that word written by a ghostly hand in the steam on my mirror?

'Of course I didn't. That young woman – she looked back at me as she did it, with such a face… Couldn't you see how shaken I was when I came in?'

'Someone who'd just committed murder might look a little shaken, too.'

'I've met some murderers,' replied Winston, 'doing the work that I do. And they're as likely to seem relieved and light-hearted as contrite.'

'You don't seem either of those things,' said James.

'Exactly, because I haven't killed anyone!'

'If you didn't kill Bella and Ravi, then who did?' James challenged him.

'You did! And if I can't persuade the young lady to come here to me, you'll do it again before the police arrive.'

'You think for one second I'm going to put her in your hands?'

'It's my choice to make!' They both looked meek and waited for me to speak again. 'Winston, I don't see how anyone but you could have done it. I trust James. I'm not leaving him.' My voice was strong and sure, much more so than my heart. But it was what I had to believe.

Winston shrugged and sighed.

'I suppose I've never been much of a one for saving people. And I won't be starting now. Do give a blood-curdling shriek, though, when you find you were wrong.'

Then he turned and headed back down the stairs, out of sight.

CHAPTER 22

'Damn.'

I looked enquiringly at James.

'He's gone to the kitchen. Now we can't even get a cup of tea.'

My first instinct was to disapprove. We were feet away from Bella's body, and the sweet metallic tang of blood was thick in the air. How could he think of breakfast? But the insistent gnaw of my own stomach stopped me. We hadn't eaten anything since yesterday teatime, and we'd drunk a lot on top of that. It was an empty, acidic mess in there, and hunger was beginning to make it hard to think straight. Then inspiration struck.

'Snacks for the trip! I had a couple of chocolate bars in my bag, but then I felt a bit queasy on the ferry, so I didn't eat them.'

James looked at me as though I'd suddenly grown longer

legs or bigger boobs, or whatever it was that did it for him –
I realised I didn't really know.

'Chocolate bars?'

'Yup.'

'Good ones? With nuts in?'

'Yup.'

'If I hadn't already kissed you, now's the time I'd start.'

I laughed and turned to lead the way to my room. I didn't
look back, but my smile slipped as I thought of what was
behind us in the hall. Bella. So beautiful; so fiercely aware of
what she was owed as a beauty; so loyal to Ravi; now slumped
forward, her perfect face lacerated, her eyes empty of any
light, fixed on the pool of her own blood.

In the Peach Pit, as James christened it, I gave him one
chocolate bar and snaffled my own while I hunted through
my bag for a matching pair of socks.

'What do you think we should do?' he asked, around a
mouthful of chocolate.

'Is there anything we can do? Besides barricade ourselves
in one of these rooms and wait for the police?'

'Maybe not. But I feel like we need to take action, resist
what's happening somehow.'

I sat down to put my socks on and then finished the
chocolate, letting the sensory delight of warm feet and sugary
tongue fill my mind, not hunting for an answer. I admired
James's active personality, but it had always been more my style
to retreat under a duvet and wait for a problem to go away.
I didn't think I was the person to save us from a crazed killer.

'We could build a bonfire!'

Nourishment was calming me down, but he seemed more and more excited. His eyes were shining, and he hopped up and began to pace the room, stuffing the last bites of chocolate into his mouth and talking around them.

'A big enough fire might be seen from the next island. We could look for wood in the sheds. There's got to be a supply; this house is full of fireplaces.'

'But aren't the police on their way already? Is anyone going to get to us faster?'

'Maybe not, maybe not.' It sounded like he was conceding the point, but I got the impression he wasn't really listening to me that closely. He kept pacing, now licking the last traces of sugar from his fingers. 'Still, we've got to try something. Something big, something bright. The storm has broken; haven't you noticed? The light will travel. It's worth a try.'

'I guess... Not to be a naysayer, but there's something else. It's New Year's Day, right? Won't people just think it's a late bonfire? That Hogmanay hasn't quite ended on this island?'

'You can't just go through life assuming the worst, Millie. Sometimes you just have to try things, take the leap, see where you end up.'

He was standing in front of the window now, rocking back and forth on his feet, looking out and rubbing his hands in anticipation. This sudden energy made me nervous; I wondered if he was in some kind of shock from seeing Bella's body. Or if he'd dipped into his bag of party supplies to soften the horror.

'Surely looking before you leap is the more relevant maxim in a situation like this?'

'What? Oh yes, very clever. But you can't just wait for your fate to come for you. We're sitting ducks here with that killer downstairs. We've got to take action; we've got to resist.'

I could have told him that ducks are actually tough to hunt, but with his wild eyes and his vehemence, I felt suddenly nervous of contradicting him. I decided I'd just go along with it. Building a fire would be cold, windy and, as far as I could see, pointless, but it probably wouldn't do any harm either. And it would be a distraction from sitting in this room, waiting for the police and waiting for Winston to come for us.

'Fine, but at least let me brush my teeth properly first. I still feel grubby from last night.'

I grabbed my binoculars on my way into the bathroom, hoping for some reason that James wouldn't notice. I did want to brush my teeth – and to wash my face, which, I saw in the mirror, had the shiny pallor of a suet pudding after my broken, drunken sleep. But I also wanted to scan the sea for boats. With Bella dead now, too, I had begun to feel very afraid.

I flipped off the lens caps and focused the glasses. It was still half-dark outside, an exhausted grey that indicated the storm had caused as much havoc outside as the whisky had in. *Please let there be lights coming. Red and blue lights.* I ran my gaze over the horizon, back and forth, fervently hoping – but there was nothing. Even the birds seemed to be lying low this morning; I didn't see a single dark shape winging across the dim sky.

'Come on!' James pounded against the bathroom door. 'The fire will be more visible right now; we don't want to wait for full light.'

'Just a second!' I scrubbed at my teeth for a few seconds and dashed more water on my face. *No improvement*, said the mirror. I grimaced at myself and went out. James was pacing by the door, still jittery and in a fever to be doing something. I shrugged on my jacket. 'Have you heard anything from downstairs?'

'No, and I don't like it. The more I think about it, Millie, the more I realise he must have brought us all here for a reason. It was all so… orchestrated.'

'You mean, not just murders on the spur of the moment?'

'No, no crimes of passion. Think of the fuss he made about the double-booking that first night. He's been playing a game all along. But listen.' He took me by the shoulders and, standing still at last, looked me hard in the face. 'We won't let him win it. You and I, we're getting off this island. Together.' And he pulled me into his chest, crushing me against it in an embrace so tight I couldn't breathe.

James wanted to check the outbuildings for firewood, or anything flammable we could make into a pyre.

'Though to be honest,' he remarked as we passed the library door on our way outside, 'a lot of this furniture deserves to be burned anyway.'

We went around the building to get to the sheds, passing by the kitchen window. Winston was standing there now, and I thought of the last time I'd looked through the window from this side, on the night we'd arrived. I'd been with James then, too, and, then as now, the person looking back at us had seemed frightened. But Mrs Flyte had been frightened for herself, and I could see from the concerned kink between his brows that Winston was worried for me. Or at least that he was trying to look like it. He shook his head slowly as we walked by, as though he couldn't believe my foolhardiness.

'Just ignore him. He's been messing with our heads from the start. Don't give him the satisfaction of paying it any mind.'

The outbuildings were clustered together, strangely close, I thought, given the empty space available on the island. But I realised as we navigated the warren of paths between them that the crowding kept them more or less sheltered from the wind. I had been out here before, when I took a walk in the growing storm. It was only the previous afternoon, but it felt like several lifetimes ago. And, in a way, it was – two lives had been lost since then. And now I was afraid for my own.

I hadn't paid much mind to the sheds the day before. I had been too preoccupied with my own thoughts and the cold wet misery of being out in the storm. Now it was still too dark, in the slowly dawning day, to see much of them. I tested a few handles, but everywhere was locked.

'Over here! I found an open one.' James, a few metres ahead of me on the path, ducked into a dark doorway. 'Did you bring your phone or something? Can't see my own feet.'

I reached the door and peered inside. As James had indicated, there was very little light, and I could only gain a shadowy sense of the space within, grey shapes hinting out of the dark.

'There's something here. Help me.' James was scrambling on the ground, and when he came up and moved back towards the door, I saw his hands were full of paper. 'What are these?'

To my surprise and alarm, I knew.

'I've seen them before. They're profiles of the guests. All of us.'

'What? Like dossiers on who we are?'

'Yeah, really creepy. But they weren't here when I last saw them; they were on Mrs Flyte's desk.'

'Why didn't you tell me about this?'

I shrugged.

'People were dying. And then we… There were just a lot of distractions. It kind of slipped my mind.'

'Jesus, Millie. It's a big thing to forget about.' He was close to shouting now, breathing heavily and working the papers over with his hands. 'If I'd known about this, if I'd known before…'

'What? You'd have swum to the mainland? You'd have been able to save Bella? What difference could it have made?'

'I don't know. But it shows this whole thing was planned, and I'm not going to let that plan be carried out. Stay here if you're too afraid to try and save yourself!' And he stormed away, gravel flying off to either side where his feet struck the path.

'Fuck.'

I leaned against the nearest wall and slid down until I was sitting on the ground. How had I ended up in this position again, one day later, crouching by the sheds and crying? And how had things degenerated so quickly between me and James? My shoulders shook and my face grew hot and slick as I thought about last night, the island of sweet companionship we'd briefly inhabited. Now, again, I was in the water. Alone.

I tried to take deep breaths and calm my tears. *It's not so bad*, I told myself. But another voice replied immediately: *Are you kidding? There are three dead bodies in the house. It's really bad!* In a strange way, though, this comforted me, at least regarding my argument with James. Of *course* we were shouting at each other; this was a crazy situation, and tensions were running high.

Should a new boyfriend really be your top priority right now? But I was done listening to nagging little inner voices. I was afraid for my life. Someone was killing people on this island; it was a more obvious threat than before, maybe, but I had been dying a slow death all year. Death by isolation. The thought of going back to my lonely life in my messy flat with its grey city light and the same view of the ugly building across the street, the same view that I had stared at every day since I lost my job – that was as scary as anything waiting for me inside the house. I wanted to live, but I couldn't bear to live that life. I needed someone. I would go back in and make it up with James, and if he wanted to do some crazy thing like building a bonfire or barricading Winston into his room, I would do it with him. No questions asked.

I gathered the fallen papers from the shed floor, straightening them into a pile: something I could bring back as a peace offering. I wiped my eyes and, carrying the dossiers before me, headed back towards the house.

As I started back, I nearly stumbled over a horrible thought: would James still be alive when I got there? While I had been crying over my lonely lot and deciding whether or not to make it up with him, he had been rushing towards a confrontation with a double, possibly a triple, quadruple, or worse, murderer. A serial killer. My steps and my heartbeat quickened, and I was nearly running by the time I made it up the path to the steps. But my fears were quickly allayed. James opened the door just as I reached it. He looked a bit flattened; maybe he, too, had been feeling regret about the tiff.

'Millie…'

'No, let me say something. I'm sorry I didn't keep you in the loop with everything. It was stupid and untrustworthy, and I wish I could go back and do things differently. Because I do trust you. I think I have since we met on the boat. And I don't want the past few minutes to ruin what came before. It was really important to me. *You're* really important to me.'

'Oh, Millie.' He looked infinitely sad, and my stomach started to give way.

'Now's the part when you say, "You're really important to me, too."' I laughed weakly.

'You are, you are. It's not that, it's…' He seemed to struggle for a moment, trying to find the right words, and then he gave up and opened the door a little wider, stepping aside so I could see.

Behind him.

Winston, hanging from the antler chandelier.

Dead.

And only James could have killed him.

CHAPTER 23

We were still for what seemed a very long time. James and I were still, that is; Winston swung gently back and forth, stirred by the wind, not too strong now, blowing in from the door.

He looked somehow deader than any of the bodies I'd seen in the past twenty-four hours. Bella and Ravi had been bloodier, but there was something terribly inert about Winston, dangling there in the centre of the hall.

The sharp arcs of the cracked antlers pointed upwards, and, caught among their prongs, the rope that held him pulled heavily down. His face, above the noose, was swollen by suffocation, tongue pressing pinkly out of his mouth. Horribly, one of his hands was still caught up in the rope where he must have scrabbled at his neck while dying. As his body turned in the draught, I saw that his snowy hair was reddened at the back with blood.

'Did you hit him on the back of the head to do it? So you could put him in the noose unconscious?'

I wasn't sure why I broke the silence with that remark. Surely, I should be running away, screaming? But my feet had forgotten how to move, and who was there to scream for, anyway? Out of the seven people who had been on this island when I arrived, there was only me left. And James. The murderer.

It made sense; of course it did. My taste in men had led to trouble before. And then, James had never quite been able to explain himself. I thought of that conference in the kitchen, after Ravi died. The rest of us had all had normal, traceable connections to each other. But not him. He'd always stood apart.

But, as obvious as the truth was now, he was still trying to deny it.

'Millie, no. I didn't do this. Please…' His eyes were large with anguish, and he put a hand out to me, but dropped it, warned by something in my face. 'I know this looks bad, but I swear, I found him like this as soon as I came back in. I didn't do it!'

'It's no use, James.' Still, I couldn't persuade my feet to move. My voice emerged calm and flat, less scared than disappointed. 'It couldn't be anyone but you. The others are all dead. Everyone.'

'I don't know how to explain it. It seems impossible to me, too. Maybe Bella was right about resentful spirits?' He gave me a desperate, cringing smile, as though abashed by the lameness of the excuse. Unexpectedly, I smiled back at him.

'Sure. And the dog ate your homework, right?'

What are you doing? I asked myself. And the answer came back surprisingly quickly, as though the gears of my mind had finally begun turning again. *Keeping him on side. Don't you want to get out of here alive?*

The part of me that had acted before I could think was right. I had to keep him sweet until the police arrived. He might have a prosthetic leg, but he was taller, fitter and stronger than I was. Unless… That leg. I thought about the hitch in his step when we walked up the path from the dock, about his stumble in the kitchen when he spilled the scrambled eggs.

'We should build a bonfire, like you said.' He looked confused at the change of subject. 'The wind's died down. And the rain too. It'll burn beautifully, and we want to get off this island, don't we?'

'Sure, but aren't you – I mean…' He gestured at the slowly turning body behind him.

'Like you say, vengeful ghosts.'

'Millie, I'm glad you don't think it's me, but I didn't mean that. I don't understand how, but someone else must be hiding themselves on this island. We're still in danger.'

'All the more reason to build a bonfire. Come on, grab some wood from the fireplace. I've got kindling.' I gestured at the papers, still in my hands. He looked at me, still a little perplexed, and then walked off to the library, carefully averting his face from Winston's corpse.

I stared at it while he was gone, thinking how sick it was he was trying to get me to play along with his false innocence, and even sicker, maybe, that I was willing to do so. How repugnant that he wouldn't look at a man whose life he had stolen. I was steeling myself against him. I would need to think only of this James for my plan to work. Not the James of last night. Not the James who had cooked for everyone without complaining. Who had smiled and struck up a friendly conversation with me on the ferry. Whose cosy flannel shirt was still protecting me from the wind. That warmth and kindness – it had all been an act. Designed to pull us in, lull us into trusting vulnerability. But as those moments flashed through my mind, I still felt the pull of his charm.

God, I felt stupid. He'd warned me himself, in a way, telling me about his dark-web activities. He'd claimed it was because he could relate to people in pain, but who knew what those pills were used for at the other end? Maybe he'd been an accessory to murder many times over already. And the people on this island, the people he'd killed, they were just the next step in a murderer's progress.

Suddenly signs came back to me, clues I should have noticed at the time. The cat locked in the cupboard: he'd been quick to say the lock could have turned on its own, as though he didn't want us examining it too closely, as though he already knew the cupboard well.

My God. Ravi. Winston had pointed it out to me, and I should have listened then: whoever killed Ravi would have had to walk past Bella to get to the door. She must have been telling the truth about waiting on that chair for her anger to pass. It was only me who had invaded Penny's room, even if I had found it unlocked. But no one had come up the stairs carrying that axe. James must have taken the weapon while Winston slept, waited in the broom cupboard, emerged to kill Ravi and hidden there again, until Bella went in and he could sneak past and go downstairs. Only to appear a few minutes later, all innocent bewilderment.

Now he was coming back, arms full of stacked logs, looking at me a little warily. And he wasn't wrong to be wary.

'We should go to higher ground, closer to the water,' I said. 'So we can be sure any passing boat will see the fire.'

'Where were you thinking?'

'The place Penny died. It seems fitting, somehow.'

'And it's on the right side of the island for boat traffic. Let's go.'

He moved ahead of me up the path. I was watching for a stumble as though for a sign; it was him or me now, and I wasn't sure I could trust myself to do what needed to be done. I needed some extra weight in the balance, one more thing to tip me over.

At the crest of the hill, where we had found the bundle of Penny's clothes, just by the cliff edge, we dropped to our knees and started building a fire. I didn't look over the brink. Penny's body had either washed away or been battered to a point I couldn't bear to see. Nor did I want to be reminded of just how far down it was to the rocks.

'Should we really be burning those?' I stopped the automatic twisting of my hands, recalled by James's voice. 'I mean, aren't they evidence or something?'

'You're right.' I had turned half the pile of documents into rough spills to use as firestarters. I smoothed the crumples out of the sheets. 'Some of these are just scrap paper, though. I'll sort them: you go and get more wood. We want this fire to be visible from far away.'

He stood and started moving off, but before he disappeared down the slope, I called:

'Wait.'

He was the only person left who could possibly have killed everyone. I knew that, and yet a tiny flicker of hope had just flashed through my heart when he stopped me from burning the files. Surely a murderer would want all evidence of his crimes erased? And yet there was no way – no way that I could see – that he wasn't the killer.

All I could do now was ask a question that might throw him off balance, make the mask slip, if he was wearing one. I thought of what I'd asked Winston when I believed that he'd murdered Bella, the one thing, it had occurred to me at the time, that really mattered to me. I looked at James and hoped I would be able to see the truth in his face. Whether it was the truth I wanted or not.

'On the cliff here, when Penny died… Did you push her?'

'Oh, Millie.'

He was reaching for me, and I could see an awful sadness and sense of betrayal in his face.

He didn't, I thought. Somehow, he didn't. My heart swelled, and I was reaching for him, too.

But before our hands could meet – *BANG!*

CHAPTER 24

Blood and brain and bone. His head exploding, spraying across my vision. The gunshot deafening me.

It hadn't been him. He hadn't been the killer. I was getting ready to push him off the cliff edge, exploit that slight instability of his prosthetic leg. Kill him. And for no reason. He wasn't the killer.

But he *was* dead.

James was behind me now, lying where he'd fallen on the heathery ground. I was running, and thinking that he was dead, and not seeing anything I passed, because my head was full of the vision of his head exploding into bone and brain and blood.

I hadn't seen the person shooting him. He had been standing on a rise, looking towards me at the cliff edge, and the shot had come from behind and below him, the shooter hidden by the slope. But I knew who had done it, as impossible as it seemed.

I had seen the swirl of Winston's coat, far away by the time I stood up and made it past James's body, retching and crying, to where I could see.

He had been running back towards the house, distant but recognisable by his beautiful long camel coat, which I had so much admired in the moments before he announced Penny's suicide. I was running after him, no longer retching, though tears were still seeping out of my eyes, only to be plucked quickly away by the wind.

Why was I running after him? Surely I should stay as far away as I could.

Only, James was dead. And he hadn't been the killer.

Meaning I hadn't been wrong to start falling for him.

Meaning we could have had a future together.

For a second, I stopped, bent over and gasping. I was out of breath from running, but it was that realisation that had punched me in the gut. Whatever future there might have been for us was gone.

And if I wasn't careful, my own future would be gone, too. I was the only one left alive on the island. Just me and Winston. And it seemed safe to assume he wanted to kill me.

I really wasn't sure how to avoid getting killed. For the tenth time in the past two days – for the thousandth time in the past year – I wanted to sob. I was trapped alone on an island with a crazed murderer, completely out of ideas for escape. A terrible weekend to cap off a disappointing life.

But I didn't collapse. I stood up and set off running towards the house again. Winston was out of sight, but there was nowhere else on this empty little rock for him to go. And I was damned if I was going to let him hunt me down as he had done the others. We'd been dancing to his tune this whole time, always being led. It was time for a record scratch, time to bring him out into the open.

I could see from the steps leading up to the door that Winston's body was no longer hanging from the chandelier. Of course, it couldn't have been; otherwise, how could he have come after us and killed James? But he had looked so very dead and gone. I had half-expected to find him hanging still, even though I'd also seen him running away from James's murder, coat flapping dramatically behind.

Whatever he'd done to get himself up there in order to play dead, it had obviously been trickier coming down. The antler chandelier was smashed on the tiles of the hall, cracked by age and impact into several many-pointed splinters. I stood in the doorway for a minute, then another, surveying the wreckage and listening to my heart slow. When my breathing was calm – or as calm as could be expected, walking into a house that contained my prospective murderer – I stepped gingerly over the threshold.

At each step forward, I paused, straining to hear any indication of movement from the other rooms. Then I thought of my impulse to turn the tables, and I strode quickly over to the gong that the cat had so frightened us with. Before I could think better of it, I picked up the mallet and gave it a huge whack.

Before the *crasssshhhh* had finished resounding, I heard heaving footsteps running overhead.

'So, you're upstairs, are you?' I shouted. 'Here I come.'

My courage lasted as long as it took to bound up the stairs, and then, at the top, I remembered: he had a gun. *Shit*. My legs did my thinking for me, and I dropped to all fours, hugging close to the banister. Suddenly it didn't seem like such a good idea to bring my enemy out in the open.

The steps had seemed to come from the northern end of the upper floor, so I turned down the part of the corridor that ran south. Crawling alongside the wall, I kept looking over my shoulder. I crept around the corner and, when I came to a door, I reached up, twisted the handle and half-fell over the threshold, praying I wouldn't find Winston already there.

For a moment I remained glued to the door, wrapped in a ball, my eyes tight shut. I heard nothing but my own raucous breathing. Eventually, I dared to open first one eye, then the other. I looked around.

At first, I thought I was alone. Nothing but my own breath disturbed the air of the silent room. Around me was a clutter of clothing, papers, knick-knacks and books. I was in Mrs Flyte's room, and her body was still on the bed.

As I realised this, I gave a little horrified moan. I clapped my hand over my mouth, listening for footsteps coming down the hall. Nothing. I hoped I was too far away from Winston for him to have heard.

I tried to gather myself back together, to find the courage that had crashed against that gong and carried me up the stairs. But it was nowhere inside me. The thought of the shotgun had blown it away. I remained huddled against the door, breathy and trembling, trying not to look too closely at the sheet-shrouded form on the bed.

I had to think through the fear. What did I have that I could use against Winston? Very little, other than the knowledge the police were on their way, which in my current position seemed a frail hope. But it was the only hope I had. If I was going to survive, I had to play for time, making sure he couldn't hurt me before that boat came.

So, how to stall him? The trouble was that Winston was smarter than me. In retrospect, it should have been obvious that he was the killer. He was much the cleverest person in the group, the most slyly observant of the rest of us. He had worn his hostility on his sleeve from the beginning, too, with his sharp remarks and interrogations. He'd avowed his own motive, at least as far as Ravi was concerned. And now it occurred to me that he was the only one of us, besides Mrs Flyte, who hadn't been invited by some mysterious third party. In spite of his obfuscations about the booking mix-up, he had admitted intending to come here. No one had been in a better position, or more naturally suited, to manipulate and destroy the rest.

Though why he wanted to kill any of us still escaped me. Ravi, sure. And perhaps Bella and Mrs Flyte were just collateral damage, people who couldn't be kept out of it, pawns he'd been willing to sacrifice. But why the rest of us? And why such a brutal death for Bella, if she wasn't his real target? I had passed her collapsed form during my crawl down the corridor and had carefully avoided lifting my eyes above her oddly bent ankles. Why James? Why me? Whatever the reason, he clearly wanted to make us suffer. There was no other cause to hide from me now; he was just drawing out the torture.

Part of the clutter stretched and stirred. My heart stopped, but only briefly. It was the damned cat again. He had been curled up in the clothes on the floor, and now he rose and clawed at his resting place, twitching his tail and sending a spasm through each reawakened limb. Picking his way carefully around the detritus on the floor, he headed towards me.

Maybe he just wants to be stroked. Quietly. But of course, he didn't. He wanted out of the room, and after pawing at me, then at the door, and finding both curiously resistant to his will, he began to meow.

'Shh! You're going to get me killed!' I hissed.

'*Mraaaouuu*,' he replied, complaining louder.

Then I heard a step. Or thought I did, faintly, far down the hall. The cat was drowning out other sounds and burrowing into my side, trying to get through me to the door. I pushed him forcefully away.

'Shut up!' He stalked off, tail high, quiet for the moment, projecting a complete indifference to the whole question of the door.

There was definitely another step. And another. They came cautiously closer, one foot falling, a pause, then the next. I cringed against the door. My eyes were fixed on the cat, which was licking a paw with heartless nonchalance. He looked up, and straight at me, green eyes flaring though the dim room. There was something malevolent in that gaze.

As though he wanted me to be found and that was the real reason he'd started yowling.

All the time, the steps came closer.

Now they were here. Outside. I bit my fist, hard enough to break the skin. It took everything I had not to cry out. I heard feet shifting on the other side of the door, strangely high-pitched breathing. Any second he would come through that door and end me.

Images flashed up behind my tightly shut eyelids: James leaning in to kiss me last night; the Flights team popping champagne when we had a conservation win; my dad pointing silently at the sky. Anything good to hang on to from my life, so that the last thing I saw before that door opened and I died wasn't a hostile cat licking itself next to a dead body under a sheet.

The doorknob didn't turn. The feet moved off, suddenly striding purposefully down the hall. They stopped, then a moment later they ran back again and past my hiding place. I heard them pounding down the stairs and out of the door, after which they were lost to my ears.

The cat wandered back over, and this time I let him out.

'Much good may it do you.'

He stalked off, untouched by my spite.

Winston must have heard me breathing on the other side of the door. Mustn't he? I could hear him. Why had he left, when he had me right there?

Wanting to see what he had seen, I carried on walking down the corridor away from him, in the direction he had first taken after pausing at my door. Past the chair where

Bella claimed to have sat and not noticed whoever went into her room to kill Ravi. Past Winston's door, past James's, and past others I hadn't looked behind at all. At the end of the corridor was a window, and on the deep ledge I saw my binoculars.

How dare he take those from my room? was my first thought, but then it occurred to me to wonder what he'd been looking at. Something had made him leave me behind in my hiding place and run out of the house. I snatched at the glasses. My heart was thumping in my throat, my fingers trembling, too clumsy to focus the lenses. Finally, I trained my gaze on the horizon and – yes – unbelievably, my hope was realised.

There was a pulsing flash, faint but getting stronger, of red and blue lights.

The police boat was on its way.

I lowered the glasses because I couldn't see through them any more; tears of relief were clouding my view. But I caught a ripple through the window, something moving, much closer than the boat.

The tail of Winston's coat, disappearing around the far corner of the house as he ran towards the pier where they would land.

But why would he want to go and meet them? Surely he wasn't demented enough to try and kill them, too?

No. He wasn't. But he might be demented enough to try and get away with what he'd done by telling them that I did it. Demented enough to try and, worse, clever enough to succeed.

Now my own feet were pounding along the hall towards the stairs, flying down them two at a time, leaping across the tiles to the door. And with each step a question came back, an implication, a lifted eyebrow – every suggestion Winston had ever made in the conversations we'd had these past two days, that the strange goings-on could be my doing. Now I realised he'd been laying a breadcrumb trail of blame, leading to this moment. I couldn't let him be the one waiting at the jetty.

I flew around the corner of the house, part-way down the hill towards the pier, then skidded to a stop when I saw there was nobody there. I looked behind me, turning fast enough to make myself dizzy, scanning the hilly line of the island. Then I saw – a figure silhouetted against the diffused brightness of the overcast sky, waving at me from high above. I ran after him, not sure what his game was, but knowing I had to stop him, I had to be the one to tell the police what happened.

I caught up on the cliff side of the island, just out of sight of the landing dock. I say caught up, and I mean it in both senses. I stopped running and bent over a few feet away, no longer needing to chase. And I understood who it had been, wearing Winston's coat, preparing my death or arrest. Who had been playing this game all along. Not Nick. Not Bella. Not James. Not Winston.

They were all innocent.

But Penny wasn't.

CHAPTER 25

For a moment, all I could do was stare at her. I didn't doubt, now that she was standing in front of me, that she was the person who had been running the show. In spite of the many different accusations I'd made over the course of the weekend, the wildly diverging interpretations of my plight that I'd believed in at one point or another, I didn't expect another twist in the tale after this. Seeing her there, wearing Winston's coat, holding the shotgun, things clicked into place with a rightness that had been missing from my understanding of the situation all along. Who else would have known to play on my feelings for Nick to lure me out here? Only Penny. It had always been Penny.

But still, I had thought she was dead until a minute ago. My mind had been whirling for two days; it needed a beat to settle.

This wasn't what Penny was expecting. She stood there, chest heaving, challenging me with her gaze. Her eyes were mean, and her fingers worked on the barrel of the gun. It wouldn't take much to set her off. She must have been waiting for me to gasp, or faint, or start accusing her dramatically, because when I'd been quiet for a minute, just trying to still my mind and think back over the signs I should have noticed from the past few days, she decided to break the silence.

'So, here we are.'

'Together again.'

Her mouth gave a bitter twist.

'And for the last time.'

'What do you mean, "the last time"?' It was obvious what she meant, but I was stalling – better to make her walk me through it.

'Well, this.' She patted the gun. 'You die. I run screaming to the police about to land and explain how you killed everyone else and then yourself.'

'Jesus Christ, Penny. What did I ever do to you?' Again, a question I knew the answer to. I was walking a fine line. I had to keep her talking, but not enrage her with my obtuseness. For the moment, I seemed to have kept to the right side of it.

'What did you ever do to me? What did any of them ever do to me? I suppose ruining my life wasn't much to any of you. But it meant a hell of a lot to me.'

She looked desolate, saying this, and I felt a momentary twinge of guilt, the same contrition that had filled me when confessing to James. But then – James. The guilt evaporated, and anger rushed in to fill its place.

'All right, fine. I'll admit I wasn't such a great friend to you. But the others? You didn't even know them. And the Strangs died in a car crash. You're not going to tell me you did that, too?' Even as I said it, though, it occurred to me that she'd convinced us she was dead, so maybe spooky action at a distance wasn't so far beyond her.

She gave a low laugh. It was very disturbing from someone holding a gun, someone who's said they plan to kill you.

'You're right. The Strangs I didn't kill. Even though they started it all.'

'What do you mean?'

'Oh, Millie.' She turned and looked out to sea. I edged along a few inches, trying to get farther inland than she was. I thought she might be looking out for the police boat, but when she turned back there were tears in her eyes. They welled onto her cheeks and were whipped away in little beads by the wind, joining the salty ocean spray. 'I was so happy at Flights, for a while. Even if I didn't have the bird thing, like you.'

'More of a cat person.'

'That's true.' Her laugh was a little less frightening, this time. 'But we were a good team, weren't we? You and me. And Nick, even if his pranks were idiotic. And the Strangs.'

'You mean Drew, really.'

'No, it was both of them. I fell in love with both of them, in a way. I mean, I was only sleeping with him, but it was the effect of the two of them together that turned my head.

I guess I thought I could be inside it, somehow, as his mistress. Don't you remember, Millie, how beautiful they were together?'

'Yes. A pair of black swans.'

'That's it. Glossy and proud. Even when I got pregnant, I wasn't trying to take him away. But I wanted something of my own. And they wouldn't let me have it. Always going on about their conservation efforts and the reputation of the charity.' Her hands tightened around the stock of the gun. 'Shutting me out. It was like school again. Like Ravi and Bella.'

'You knew them at school?' I had known this; Bella had mentioned it. But in the subsequent bloody mayhem it had slipped my mind.

'Oh yes. I knew them. Very, very well.' She looked out to sea again, and I stepped another inch landward. 'Not that you'd have known it from the way they blanked me when they got here.'

'You didn't let on either.'

'I haven't spoken to them in twelve years. Not since Ravi filmed me having sex with him, and Bella posted it online.'

'When you were all at school together?' I could see how this might still sting. How it might ruin a life, even. And they had kept doing it, Bella had implied. Death might be a harsh punishment for some adolescent bullying, but for a lifetime of selfish exploitation? Maybe it wasn't so unfair.

'They were beautiful then, too. Well, you saw. And I was always so dull. I just wanted a little of it to rub off on me. I'm not dull now, though, am I?'

'No. No one could accuse you of that.'

'Anyway, it hurt a little. Or a lot. And then, years later, another couple, the pattern repeating again. I thought Lorna had accepted the situation. I thought she was happy to share. I didn't expect to have all of him. Even most of him. But I did want his baby. When I got pregnant, they both came down on me, saying I couldn't have it. And when I refused to terminate, they decided to terminate me. That's where Winston comes in.'

'He didn't seem to know you either.'

'He didn't know me to look at. Or even by name. But he did help them fire me.'

'How?'

'You can't just get rid of a pregnant employee, can you? All kinds of legal trouble can ensue. So, they got advice from someone they could trust. Someone who wasn't too scrupulous. He and Drew went way back – some kind of old boy network. And I saw the emails where they wrote to each other about legitimate excuses for sacking me. Just referring to me as "X". They weren't even smart enough to hide it properly.' She finished with a smug smile.

'But what about James? He had nothing to do with Flights. And he was from Scotland; you can't have gone to school with him too.'

'No, you're right. James was quite different. All those people, the way they hurt me, it gave me a past. But James… James stole my future.' She stopped, letting the wind take a few more angry tears. I puzzled over what she'd said, and then it clicked into place.

'The baby. He sold you something online.'

'And he didn't explain...' Her voice caught, but this time I waited for her to pick up the thread. 'Do you have any idea what it's like to lose a child? Not even emotionally. Just what you have to go through physically?'

'Penny, I'm sorry you had to experience that, but what you're doing now –' I was cut off by the low laugh, back and creepier than ever.

'No, you don't understand. I was too late to get an abortion. And you and I, out all night drinking, you telling me I had to get rid of it... I found James, and I took his pills, but I'm not a doctor. The dose was off, and the baby was further along than it should have been for that. It didn't work like it was supposed to. Maybe if it had...' She shifted the gun to her other hand so she could rifle around in Winston's pocket. Eventually she held up a large white handkerchief, neatly pressed. 'I knew he'd have something like this.' She blew her nose and wiped her eyes. While she wasn't looking, I edged farther away from the cliff. She was almost between me and it now.

'I had to go to hospital, in the end. When a baby dies late in the second trimester you have to give birth to it. I wasn't thinking. I was expecting to do everything at home and cover it up. If you thought Ravi and Bella lost a lot of blood...' I shuddered, and hoped she'd take it for a shiver in the January wind. 'Things went south, and when I woke up, well, let's just say that was the one and only time I'll experience labour.'

'Oh Penny, that's awful.'

'It is, isn't it?' She gave an odd, brisk smile, as though the next thing out of her mouth would be, 'Ah well, mustn't grumble.' Instead, she said, 'That's why I wanted you all to suffer, too.'

'That's why you've been doing this, then? Revenge?'

'I had planned to be more merciful, really. I was going to get you all out here, confront you, and let you go once you'd made an embarrassed apology. And if you didn't seem contrite? Well, no one would taste the poison in Marjorie's cooking, would they?'

'What changed?'

'The Strangs. A stupid accident. The people who deserved to suffer most, who had the most to make up for… They were out of it before I could even confront them. It didn't seem fair. And then Ravi and Bella ignored me. I sat up late with Winston the night you arrived, talking about you, mentioning that we'd worked together, and he didn't even make the link with the Strangs! It wasn't sitting on his conscience in the slightest, what he'd done. You all proved over and over that you were unchanged and unrepentant. You, Millie, you even rifled through my things once you thought I was dead. You were the ones who had to die.'

I shuddered a little, thinking how Penny must have been watching us from inside the house the whole time. Why hadn't we done a more thorough search? We had been scared, I suppose. And it had made us stupid.

'All right, I admit I looked through your things after I thought you were gone. But I didn't ignore you when I arrived.'

'No, and that courtesy earned you an extra day of life. I've let you stay till last.'

'But you've been playing with me. Moving Winston's body, wearing Winston's coat, that scribbled-over suicide note with my name on it, the writing on the mirror.'

She smirked.

'Good touches, no? You were so slow piecing it all together, though. I kept taking food, rearranging pictures, locking up the cat... You can't say I didn't leave hints.'

'So that was you... And the files on Mrs Flyte's desk, did you fake those so you could creep me out by strewing them around the sheds later?'

'Ah, those were real. She helped me, you see.'

'Is she alive, too?' I wasn't sure how many more resurrections I could take.

'Oh no. I killed her. But she helped me get you here, and she pretended to know nothing about it.'

'How?'

'Take Winston. I couldn't depend on a booking mix-up, could I? And what if one of you took it into your heads to write with a question about accommodation or something? She was there to make sure the illusion wasn't broken. It was easy getting you on the hook; I just had to make some fake email addresses and pick the right lure.'

'Nick.' That rage, which had died down a little as she described her ordeal with the stillbirth, flared white-hot inside me once more. I tried to stay calm, not to let it show.

'Yes, you were the easiest. All it took was a plausible fake email address. James was quite difficult. In the end I had to pay him up front – the fee he'd supposedly be getting for supplying drugs to the party.'

'What about Winston, though? It was his own idea to come here, his New Year's retreat.'

'Sure, his own idea once a promotional email mysteriously made its way to him. People have got very used to personalised ads, Millie. They don't even notice when they're a little too personalised.'

'But why would Mrs Flyte help you? She didn't seem the type to be an accomplice to murder.'

'I didn't tell her the full extent of my plan, no. But she knew I was after some kind of confrontation. Marjorie always felt guilty towards me. She didn't know how far I was planning to go, but she was willing to play along with what I told her I wanted.'

'Guilty? Towards you?'

'This is my house, really. It came to her when she divorced my father.'

I thought about what I knew of Mrs Flyte's marriage. Nothing, really, except that it had been to the kind of man who could give her a house like this in a divorce settlement. I thought of her bedroom, and of the photo of the man with the moustache, who had been talking to a child just out of view. If Penny was his daughter…

'You mean, all along, the whole time I've known you, you've been… rich?'

She snorted.

'Financially, maybe. But in other ways, I'm much poorer than you.'

Again, the rage shot through me as I thought about my year of trying to find work, watching my redundancy and savings run out, paying for the train up here, even though I could barely afford it, in the hopes that there would be some happiness waiting at the other end.

'I spent summers here as a child,' Penny carried on. 'The outbuildings, the back stairways, the old maid's rooms. None of you really bothered to look around, but there are plenty of places to hide, plenty of ways to move around without being noticed. I knew where to disappear, after Ravi, after Bella, after Winston.'

'That's why you pretended to die, then. So you could sneak around unsuspected.' She didn't contradict me. I could see that she was enjoying herself. Enjoying showing how clever she'd been. I needed to keep her talking. 'But how did you do it? It looked so real.'

'It was laughably simple, actually. There's a little ledge just under the lip of the cliff. All I had to do was make a little show for Winston, get his attention by taking off my coat, and my boots so I could climb back up easily. And then jump. He couldn't see I'd landed on the ledge, and then I climbed down and laid on the rocks. I just had to gamble on him running back to you rather than looking over the edge. If he'd looked, I'd have pulled him over, I guess. And the rest of you would just have taken a bit longer to find us.'

'But, your body on the rocks, with the rough sea... How didn't you freeze, or drown?'

'I've always been a good swimmer, ever since I was at school. And I wore a wetsuit under my clothes. But that was mostly a precaution; I barely got in the water. I just had to lie still on the rocks, until you lot had looked, and then climb back up when I was ready. Everyone was so good at jumping to the right conclusions, it worked better than I'd hoped. The most annoying part was having to retrieve my boots and coat from the house without any of you noticing. I wish you'd just left them on the cliff.'

'I was trying to be thoughtful. I was trying to act like a friend.'

'I suppose you were,' she mused. Then she hefted the gun in her hands. 'But it was definitely too little, and far too late.'

'Wait.' I racked my brain. The wind was loud in my ears, but I was pretty sure we were close enough to the dock that I'd hear the police boat. They still weren't here, and I needed more time. Which meant more questions. At last, I found a stray detail I didn't understand. 'I don't see why you'd kill Mrs Flyte. If she was willing to help you…'

'She was willing to help me get you here, but she wouldn't have been willing to help me do this. And I had reason enough to resent her, you know. She was my wicked stepmother, with a nasty streak a mile wide. The woman stole my inheritance! But even if she'd been as sweet as she liked to pretend, it had to be done, for the rest to work. And she was old, anyway. Killing her was easy. It was much more of a challenge winching Winston up to hang from the chandelier, once I'd knocked him out. With Marjorie, I just swapped her medication, and then I sat waiting in her room after my supposed suicide.'

I thought of Mrs Flyte's cagey responses when I'd questioned her in the library. So she hadn't known how far Penny was going to take things. She must have believed in the suicide and kept lying out of fear of being held responsible. But Penny hadn't finished her narration.

'She was terrified when she came in. Clutching her chest, collapsing on the floor and all that. A pillow over the face for a few seconds and she was too far gone to come back. Just alive enough for you to get to watch her die.'

'How can you talk about her like that, so coldly?'

'Because she didn't really care! None of you ever have. You just do things without any regard for who you hurt, for what damage you leave in your wake.'

She was shouting now, gesticulating with the gun. I didn't have much longer before she would snap. And I was all out of questions.

So: I ran at her and pushed.

I'd been sitting on the cliff for a good fifteen minutes before I heard the engine of the police boat pulling into the jetty and cutting out. The wind had whipped my hair into a tangle, and my hands were so cold I couldn't uncurl them. I felt calm, though, sitting in that whirl and noise. It was over.

Penny had found another ledge, but this one couldn't save her. She had landed on the gun, and it had gone off, through her. She was lying on her face, blood pooling around her, arms flung out. Not to be resurrected again.

It was so quiet with her gone, despite the wind. I sat on the cliff edge above her, enjoying the peace, waiting. I kicked my legs against the stone and thought about what I had just done, what she had just done. The black swans, gone. The couple with beautiful hair, gone. Sharp-tongued Winston, who didn't deserve to be thought a murderer. Poor, frightened Mrs Flyte, trying to make it up to her stepdaughter. And James.

James who I might have had a life with, maybe, after this. You never knew.

It wasn't the first time Penny had taken a man from me. This could all have been avoided, really. If Drew hadn't got bored.

He was just like that. Had to be seducing someone. It wasn't that Penny was more attractive than me. She was just the next in line. Still, I'd have got him back if they hadn't decided to shut down the charity. A year ago, at our New Year's party, it had been me he kissed at midnight. Not his wife. Not Penny.

Hopefully the next person I kissed at New Year's wouldn't be dead shortly after. I was getting something of a track record.

I wondered idly if Winston had taken me for Drew's discarded pregnant employee. Probably. It would have been easy to misconstrue Penny's fireside hints, and I flattered myself that I was more attractive. Piecing together what Penny said and the emails about 'X', he might easily have assumed I was the one Drew had slept with. And he wasn't wrong. But in spite of his own high rating of his intelligence, he'd misplaced his suspicions. I allowed myself a small smile of vindication.

A strong gust of wind made me wobble on the cliff edge, and suddenly I was afraid again. Was there enough evidence that Penny had been the killer to make sure I would walk free? She'd said she'd been planning to point the finger at me. How well had she laid her false trail?

There was the drafted suicide note in my pocket. I hoped she hadn't left a more explicit accusation anywhere. It didn't look good that I was the only person left alive on this island. But then, perhaps that was precisely what would save me; my story was the only one that could be told. And the police didn't need to know anything about what I'd done to Penny a year ago.

I would know, of course. I wasn't likely to forget; the shock of jealousy and anger when I realised that Penny was the reason Drew had moved on – that had seared into me. It had still been burning that night when she told me her troubles. I'd found it very soothing, ordering her drink after drink, encouraging her step by step closer to the point where she could be convinced that an abortion was her only choice. I'd remember that feeling.

But the police would only see that Penny was still clutching the shotgun, and hers would be the only prints on it. Presumably, they were on the axe, too, and on Mrs Flyte's pill bottle, although James and I had handled that as well. But we hadn't handled Winston's body, which she must have cut down and dragged away. Or written 'Guilty' on the mirror in Bella's blood.

More than that, there were the dossiers she'd prepared on everyone but herself and Mrs Flyte. I was glad, now, that I'd saved them from the fire. And the emails she'd sent to lure us here – the one from a fake address similar to Nick's real one was still in my inbox, and there would be others in everyone else's accounts, a digital paper trail leading back to Penny. Maybe there would be other online traces, too. If that video of her and Ravi shot at school were still floating around, it would support my explanation of her motive. She'd made her own opportunity, with the fraudulent invitations. And means were taken care of by the fact that she'd grown up in this house, that she knew its attics and back stairs. Now that I laid the proofs of her guilt out calmly, it was a wonder she'd thought she could get away with it at all. Maybe she hadn't. She had said that the plan was confrontation, not murder. Things just got a little out of hand. That's New Year's for you.

I could hear footsteps coming up behind me. In a second the police would arrive, and there would be questions. I was so tired. It would be difficult, a real strain, but never mind. I had the answers. There was plenty of physical evidence; it would be clear what Penny had done to the others. They'd accept my explanation. And once I had given it, I would be free. I could go home, watch some birds. Maybe start a new charity. I could name it in honour of the fallen. A Penny for the Birds. I smiled at that.

And then, as though to put nature's seal of approval on my plan, I saw something I hadn't expected: a white-tailed eagle soaring low over the rocks that tumbled from the island into the sea. It was glorious, and so close I could pick out the point of its beak, the yellow claws, the white flash of the tail. Its primaries stood out from each other, lengthening its wingspan with a flourish of sharp curves. Then it stooped for a fish, and I lost sight of it around the island.

I stretched my arms against the wind, fingers splayed like the eagle's feathers, feeling the past year blowing away. It was New Year's Day. The perfect time for a fresh start. Let old acquaintance be forgot. And never brought to mind.

ACKNOWLEDGEMENTS

Many hands, light work. My gratitude to Mark Richards and Clare Conville, each for taking a chance on me. To Bryan Karetnyk, Alex Billington and Mark Swan, for turning a manuscript into a book. To the seedplanters who worked this garden before, above all Agatha Christie, Josephine Tey, and Jonesy, who taught me the cat scare. To Jack Ramm: without you, no novel. And to Tim Smith-Laing: without you, nothing.